Shuchi Singh is the bestselling author of three popular fiction titles, *Done with Men, I Am Big. So What!?* and *A Cage of Desires*. A versatile writer, her stories span a range of subjects that are relevant to the contemporary Indian woman. Shuchi is regularly invited to universities and lit fests across India to speak on feminist issues such as body positivity, sexuality, relationships and mental health, and is also a strong voice on social media. She was recently listed as one of the top Indian women authors to follow on Twitter.

Shuchi wears many hats, each more exciting than the other. She has a full-time corporate job, is an avid traveller and is also a passionate entrepreneur with a line of aromatherapy-based natural self-care products called Saabanvali.

Shuchi Singh

RUPA

Published by
Rupa Publications India Pvt. Ltd 2020
7/16, Ansari Road, Daryaganj
New Delhi 110002

Sales Centres:
Allahabad Bengaluru Chennai
Hyderabad Jaipur Kathmandu
Kolkata Mumbai

Copyright © Shuchi Singh 2020

All rights reserved.

No part of this publication may be reproduced, transmitted,
or stored in a retrieval system, in any form or by any means,
electronic, mechanical, photocopying, recording or otherwise,
without the prior permission of the publisher.

This is a work of fiction. Names, characters, places and incidents are either the product
of the author's imagination or are used fictitiously and any resemblance to any actual
person, living or dead, events or locales is entirely coincidental.

ISBN: 978-93-5333-847-3

First impression 2020

10 9 8 7 6 5 4 3 2 1

The moral right of the author has been asserted.

Printed by HT Media Ltd, Gr. Noida

This book is sold subject to the condition that it shall not,
by way of trade or otherwise, be lent, resold, hired out, or otherwise
circulated, without the publisher's prior consent, in any form
of binding or cover other than that in which it is published.

For Ayzel...the light of my life

One

'Kay Bunny...you look err...fuller. Filling up on love, eh?' chirps Ravi as he annoyingly pokes me in the tummy with his index finger as if I'm his little brother or something. I am a woman—not a spectacularly hideous one at that either; sometimes I just wish he'd acknowledge that.

I mean he's a nice guy otherwise, but I just hate it when he inflicts all these atrocious names upon me...and the random tummy pokes. I mean you have to draw the line somewhere, don't you? I would probably not mind it all that much if I had rock-solid abs; in fact, I would be happy if someone took a moment out of their day to check them out. But sadly, those kind of abs are a distant fantasy right now—not that I ever had them anyway. His finger sinks deep into my flesh when he does that, and it just makes me cringe and suck in my breath till I can feel myself go blue in the face. Which is even more embarrassing. And 'Bunny'? Where did that even come from?

'You really still haven't grown any manners, have you, Ravi?' I say with a smile, because despite his irritating antics, I'm actually quite pleased to see him today. We are meeting after months. Ravi used to be my boss back at the New Age Traveller—NAT, but neither of us work there anymore. We've had a tumultuous equation all through, but of late, I've realized that he's the only true friend I have left in this city. Of course I have Vivian, but a girl needs her buddies too, especially since Vivian is so ridiculously busy all the time.

Ravi and I started hanging out fairly often after Baani got married last year, and he broke up with his girlfriend Ramona (which to me was no big deal since they had been together for only a few weeks and he still doesn't know her last name!). Anyway, so I was quite down and lonely after Baani left and Ravi was the only source of entertainment I had for a while.

Then of course, we both got busy with our lives...

'Forget that! What's up with you? Why are you so fat?' His tone is a little serious now and I rap him over the head. Ravi is clearly not the most charming guy I know.

You see, I started a freelance writing business soon

after I quit NAT, but all that working from home has made me—well, plump, to put it mildly. Ten freakin' kilos in ten months—can you believe it?! And that's about the only 'growth' I've had in the past year. I'm not minding the new boobs one bit, but my rear is spiralling out of control.

'I'm not FAT,' I retort defensively, 'just a little…a little…'

'FAT,' urges the Thought Bubble.

'OK, I've put on a little weight. So? And I've even joined the gym,' I say a little haughtily. Of course the gym bit is not true. I haven't seen a gym in my life, but yes, I *did* start a new diet last week and I'm feeling thinner already. The numbers haven't budged on the weighing scale but you know, inch loss?

'Oh Kay, darling. Don't get me wrong. You look fabulous as ever!' says Ravi as he pulls me into a tight hug.

'So, tell me. What's up with your life? How's Vivian?'

'Life is good, Vivian is great,' I say in between overenthusiastic nods as we both settle around a corner table by the window waiting for our coffees to arrive.

'When will I see you two lovebirds getting married?'

Shit. Why does he always have to say the wrong things at the wrong time? And to think that he's a master's in mass communication! Sometimes I fail to fathom why I even know this guy.

'It's a work in progress,' I say, nodding my head sheepishly and looking away, hoping for some sort of distraction.

'No progress happening though,' butts in the Thought Bubble, and I shush it away quickly.

Ravi is eyeing me suspiciously. 'Everything alright between the two of you?'

'Yeah, yeah of course. Everything is just perfect!' I retort, soon realizing how high pitched I sound. Not that I am insecure or anything. Just a little miffed.

See, the thing is that the wedding was supposed to have happened by now, but it didn't, for reasons best known to Vivian. Maybe he got the heebie-jeebies or something. It was quite a dampener, yes, but I guess the important thing is that we are still together and going strong. It has been almost a year since we had 'the talk' and I never brought it up ever again, hoping that he would on his own, some day. But he hasn't either. However, I can't tell all that to Ravi. He'll just think I'm a sorry pathetic loser whom no one wants to marry. Well, Vivian did say he wants to marry me 'someday', only not *right now*.

'He's just busy with work and stuff, and you know how crazy he is about starting his own hospital,' I explain as Ravi nods his head sympathetically.

It's completely true. Vivian's busy. Super busy. And I kind of feel guilty about it sometimes. I mean, he had it all going for him in Goa—the hospital and everything. And then I came into his life and there was that thing with Aisha, his partner Dr Dhawan's daughter, who tried to pry us apart (she failed miserably though, that pathetic long-legged bitch!). So, long story short, Vivian chose to leave everything behind and move to Mumbai to be with me. He has now taken up a job at Medicus Hospital, even though he hates it there.

Naturally, I have to field awkward questions from Mom, Dad and sometimes Baani about the impending change in our relationship status on a daily basis—which by the way, is getting more and more annoying. But there is little I can do about it right now.

I know he has a point about establishing himself before getting hitched, but I wish I could make my heart (and also my over-concerned parents) understand that. Apart from this little glitch, if you can call it that, all is cool in la-la land. Dating and mating rituals are being adequately complied with, moments fly when we are together, we never run out of things to talk about and we have the most fabulous bond. Except that He. Just. Won't. Get. Married!

'That's OK, at least you guys are living together,' says Ravi helpfully.

At this point, I'm beginning to get a tad overwhelmed with emotions and my chin begins to wobble as my vision becomes hazy with tears. I just can't take this anymore.

'What? What did I say? I'm sorry for whatever it is!' Ravi panics and shuffles his chair over to my side so that he can put his arm around my shoulders.

'We're...we're not living together!' I splutter, trying hard to control my sobs, and the way I say it sounds as if we've gotten divorced or something. When we're not even married!

'Aww, baby! Why? Why aren't you living together?'

'...because he somehow feels it isn't right,' I whimper like a kitten with a cold.

I don't know if it is a problem peculiar to him or if it has something to do with being on the wrong side of 30, but Vivian has rather skewed notions of morality, if you ask me. He lives a block away from my apartment, but we spend most of our time together. Or whatever is left of it, thanks to the crazy schedule he has at his new job at that fancy corporate hospital. The arrangement kinda works out for me too, given that Mom keeps dropping in every few months, but every once in a while I do daydream about us living under the same roof as...well, *a real couple*.

Ravi continues to nod but doesn't comment at all. I don't think he even gets this kind of stuff.

'He'll come around soon, don't you worry,' Ravi says finally. 'Some guys take a little longer to get into the groove. He loves you, I know it. And you two bunnies are meant to be!'

There comes the 'bunny' again. I manage a smile. Ravi knows me. He is not utterly useless after all.

My present situation doesn't feel great at all, let me tell you that. It's like sitting in a golden chariot ready to be whisked away only to find out that it has a flat tyre. Speaking of tyres, I think I should go easy on these heavenly chocolate muffins. I take a bite and pass on the rest to Ravi, who readily gobbles it up.

Frankly, I don't know where Vivian and I are heading, but I'm too scared to ask. It is like the worst thing to do to a guy who is already sitting on the fence. Who knows, he just might topple over to the wrong side. Or so says a *Cosmo* article.

'Kay Bunny, I have to go. Got a meeting to attend,' says Ravi as soon as he has gulped down his coffee, and frankly, I am in no mood to stop him because that would mean more discussions about Vivian and our seemingly non-existent future together, which I am absolutely not up for right now. I stand up to give him a hug, and he plants a peck on my forehead. Ravi and I may not find time to catch up often, but I know that despite his overwhelming annoyingness at times, he genuinely cares for me.

'I'll call you, OK?' he yells as he walks out of the café.

I quickly glug down my peach iced tea and look at the watch—it is not even noon! *Gawd, what the hell am I supposed to do all day?* I call up Vivian to ask if he'll be coming home for lunch (which is extremely rare, by the way) and as expected, he replies in the negative, but gives me a phone kiss to make me feel slightly better.

I hang around the café for a few more minutes when my phone beeps.

'Coming for the event today?'

Shit! There was supposed to be a meet-up at the Blue Cross, a rescue and rehab centre for animals, and I had promised Karan I would be there. Karan, by the way, is kind of the only person in Big Bad Bombay that I'd been socializing with—before Ravi came back, that is. He's quite cool in the sense that I can talk to him for hours and he kinda likes all the same stuff that I do—animals being one of them.

I used to go to Blue Cross every once in a while, but it was Karan who convinced me to sign up formally as a volunteer because the centre needed more hands. I really can't thank him enough for the opportunity because it makes me feel good and serves a welcome break from my lonely, cooped-up existence as a freelancer.

'Kairavi! I thought you wouldn't come!' Karan's face lights up as soon as he sees me.

'Thanks for reminding me... I had almost forgotten!' I reply morosely. He had been working hard all month to organize this fundraiser for the NGO, and I knew it would mean a lot to him if I showed up. Back when I had a full-time job, the pressure at work kind of kept me on my toes and my life was so much more organized. Now, I'm just a lump on the sofa, because quite frankly, this freelance thing isn't going all that great. It worked out fabulously for Baani, but I guess I'm not cut out for this life. And NAT won't take me back!

Two

I am right in the middle of fluffing up my evening cuppa coffee in the kitchen—I'm so addicted to caffeine these days—when a strong pair of hands grabs me from behind.

'Make one for me, will you?' Vivian whispers into my ear as he gently nuzzles my neck. I can feel his evening stubble grazing my skin and even after a year of being together, his deep voice is perfectly capable of turning my knees into jelly. I haven't seen much of him in the past two days, so I'm all too glad to make his coffee extra special. With some chocolate shavings, and all that. I beat it extra hard and even grate in some nutmeg and cinnamon. Four back-to-back surgeries, he told me. The boy could use some spicing up after a long tiring day.

'Here you go,' I hand over his cup and proceed to gently massage his shoulders. It has become sort of a routine now. It started one day when he asked me to rub his shoulders after a long day at the OT and before we knew it, had become one of our couple thingies. For all practical purposes, we are like a married couple who never quite made it to the altar. Vivian pulls me forward by the arm so I fall right into his lap. We cuddle and sip coffee as he tells me about his day.

'Kairavi, there's something really important I need to discuss with you...' he starts, his voice suddenly all serious.

Oh my God. Is he going to propose now?

'Stop imagining things in your head! Does he look like he's going to propose?' reprimands the Thought Bubble, and I land on the ground with a thud.

'What...what is it?' I ask anxiously.

'Jacinta is coming over tomorrow.'

'Tomorrow?!' I squeak.

'Yeah, sorry for springing this on you on such short notice. But she's a little upset over her divorce and really needs a break. I don't have an extra room at my place, so would you mind if she stays with you? Here?'

'Of...of course. I'd love it. Anything for you, honey!' I give him a soft peck on the cheek even though my mouth feels dry as cardboard.

Jacinta is Vivian's sister, four years older than him, and the only family he has. Oh, and did I tell you that she wasn't exactly thrilled the first time we met each other? She's this high-nosed, snooty woman who practically looks down on all of humanity, even though she is three-feet nothing. But the scary part is her influence over Vivian—he won't move a limb without her approval, not because he's scared of her, but because he feels protective and responsible towards her, especially since her marriage fell apart. I sometimes have a niggling feeling that she might have something to do with his sudden change of mind after he proposed to me a year ago at the airport. It isn't like she hates me or anything, but the way she looked at Vivian when he introduced me to her for the first time clearly said 'This one? Really now? You could have done so much better, boy!'

'Thanks, I love you!' Vivian says and hugs me tight. That's all I want—to see him happy and smiling. But Jacinta…

'Don't worry, she'll be here only for a couple of days,' says Vivian, as if he's reading my thoughts. He does that so often, it's scary.

'She's welcome to stay here as long as she likes,' I assure him, although I'm not quite sure I'd be too pleased about that.

Maybe this is my big chance to bond with Jacinta. So what if we didn't get off to a good start—I'm not going to cower and try to run away from her. She's the only family Vivian has and if I have to live the rest of my life with him, I'll have to make peace with his sister. And that's exactly what

I'll do. I can already picture the two of us going shopping together and chatting over cocktails at bars. If we become really close, we could even share clothes, like Baani and I did. Or maybe not. Jacinta has horrible fashion sense. And she's too stubby.

'Oh by the way, Ronan is coming too,' Vivian says casually and gets up to put his cup back in the kitchen.

'Ronan! Of course, how can I forget that brat!' I can hear the Thought Bubble shriek in horror. Ronan is Jacinta's three-year-old son, and he's the stuff scary movies are made of. If there was ever a 'Terrible Toddler Award', I bet my limbs it would go to him.

'Oh lovely!' I manage to exclaim with a wide smile. That little tyke—the last time we met, he pulled out a clump of my hair to save himself from falling off the sofa. I shudder at the memory.

As soon as Vivian is asleep after dinner—the poor tired soul—I sneak out of bed and begin to get the house in order. My mom always told me that people generally judge you by the way you keep your house, and I really want to make a good impression. I change the bed linen in the second bedroom, which was formerly Baani's room, but has now been taken over by Sherni, my tabby cat who occasionally craves 'her own space'—heaven knows from what! I pull the bedspread so she topples over and cover the bed with a nicer sheet. You know the Egyptian cotton ones with the high thread count? I could never really tell the difference, though. I even place a small reed diffuser by the side table, hoping against hope that Ronan won't end up knocking it over. A few silk cushions, fresh toiletries and towels in the bathroom and we're all done.

'Looks nice no, Sherni?' I ask, but Sherni just looks at me with sullen indifference. She is obviously inconvenienced because I threw her off the bed, but it's a prospective sister-in-law we're talking about here!

To be honest, Sherni is too clumsy to be a cat. You know, the other day, she tumbled out of the rocking chair for no apparent reason and kept lying on her back until I came and flipped her over? And she keeps stepping on my feet all the time. I mean cats are supposed to be graceful and sophisticated and all that…that's their whole deal isn't it? But not this one…no, sir. Sherni is more like a dog trapped in a cat's body. If it can happen with humans, I reckon it can happen with cats too. But I would love her anyway, because I love dogs just as much.

I step back and scan the room—it looks pretty decent, like one of those fancy boutique Airbnb homestays that are so in vogue these days. I'll just give it some final touches in the morning and sprinkle some room freshener. I haven't been in that room for days because it just looks so barren and desolate without Baani and her stuff.

I have to call Baani!

I immediately make myself comfortable on a chair by the window and dial her number.

'Baani!' I scream as soon as the call goes through.

'Hello, Kay?' comes a groggy voice from the other end. It is Kapil, Baani's boyfriend-of-a-decade-turned-husband. I wasn't too thrilled about him initially because he's boring as hell, but in the end, he turned out to be a pretty sweet guy. And Baani loves him to bits.

'Kapil! How are you? Where is Baani?'

'She's sleeping. What happened? Everything OK?'

Trust Kapil to get worked up over everything. 'Can't one friend call another for a quick chat,' I retort smugly.

'It's 2 a.m.!'

Oh! I got so carried away with the cleaning that I didn't bother to look at the watch.

'Uh sorry, buddy. Talk to you in the morning. Tell Baani I called. Haven't spoken to her in while.'

'You haven't really missed much,' he says in a sour voice.

'Wait, what? What do you mean "haven't really missed much"?'

'Uh nothing, she's just so bitey these days...like she'll just bite my head off!'

This guy's out of his senses. Or maybe he's high on something. Baani can never be bitey; she's the sweetest girl I know.

'She must be PMSing, dude, just go easy on her!' I offer.

'Really? She's been PMSing for the past six months! Anyway, have get up early. I'll ask her to call you. Bye.'

Weird. But then Kapil has always been a little weird, even Baani admits that. They must've had a fight or something, I reckon. But I know they'll get around it, like they always do. I still remember their wedding day—such a fun riot it was! The two of them were beaming and gleaming like a pair of phosphorescent jellyfish in a sea of gaudily dressed up seals. Baani's in-laws came to spend a few days with them right after the wedding and well, never left. Apparently that's what you get for being the perfect daughter-in-law.

I miss her now more than ever, especially since I quit my job. It just didn't feel the same anymore after the change in management. Even Ravi had left for a plum assignment in Singapore and there really wasn't much left to look forward to. In retrospect, I'm not sure if it was one of my smarter decisions. I mean NAT at least ensured that I had some kind of social life and a normal daily routine.

But on the upside, I wouldn't say I regret the decision. I've been doing a lot of stuff I'd been meaning to do all these years. First off, I work independently; I got myself enrolled as a volunteer at the Blue Cross and the few hours I spend here every alternate day are simply the best.

Three

OK, don't panic. It's only two days—you'll survive this! I keep telling myself that—some stupid positive reinforcement technique I read about in *Cosmo*—but I am really not sure if I will. Vivian is so cool and chilled out—wonder why his sister is so damn uppity about everything. I just can't believe they belong to the same gene pool, although if you look at them standing together, they look exactly the same. Like 'his' and 'her' versions of a towel. She has the same brownish hair as Vivian, and the same sharp nose. Even their teeth look the same, although I like Vivian's much better.

Oh God, she's coming up the elevator. Why is Vivian not here with me right now? Trust him to zip off to work, leaving me alone to deal with his fussy sister and her evil offspring.

'Jacinta! I'm so happy to see you,' I say in a singsong voice as I open up my arms wide to hug her. I have no idea why I had to spell out that happy-to-see-you bit. Nobody does that anymore or do they?

'Hi, Kairavi,' she says curtly and extends her arm for a handshake. Oh, no hug? OK. That's alright, I decide. I didn't really want to hug her anyway.

Ronan comes scampering from the elevator and bumps right into my thigh. *Great!* 'Heyy...look at you...all grown up!' I say as I try to plant a kiss on his cheek, but he squirms out of my grip, and starts running around aimlessly in circles like a chimpanzee on steroids.

'Grown up, eh?' smirks the Thought Bubble. But really, I'm trying to be on my best behaviour here.

'So how have you been? Long time!' I chirp as I help her settle down in the room.

'Pretty good for someone who's in the middle of a divorce,' she snaps back. I can sense the bitterness in her voice and I immediately regret asking the question. But what else are you supposed to say to a person you are meeting after six months!

The last time, we'd met at a lounge bar in Goa, but that was only for a couple of hours. It was noisy and crowded, so we didn't really get to talk to each other much. Plus, Vivian was around then to deal with her. But being home alone with her is quite another thing—it is difficult, awkward and uneasy, all rolled into one.

Minutes feel like eons as I struggle to make conversation with an unwilling Jacinta, and I am just dying for Vivian to come back. I miss him often, but I have never really *needed* him more than I do today. Somewhere deep down, I mildly hate him for doing this to me. *Doesn't he realize what a torture his sibling is?*

Soon, it's time for lunch. Vivian had mentioned (after a lot of pestering from my side) that she loves biryani, so I'd ordered in some from the best place in Bandra. Maybe that'll bring a smile to her perpetually dour face.

I'm in the middle of reheating the stuff when Ronan comes prancing into the kitchen.

'What's that?' he asks, his enormous brown eyes studying the casserole.

'It's yummy biryani. You want some?' I ask affectionately.

'Yes, Ronan wants...' he says softly. Awesomesauce! Maybe I can feed him lunch and tuck him into bed for a nap before Jacinta comes out of the shower. She'll be so thankful!

I'm busy picturing myself feeding Ronan and telling him stories on the dining table when I hear a crash. I am snapped out of my reverie, only to find all the biryani scattered over the floor.

'Fuck! Fuck! Fuck!' I yell as I proceed to clean up the nice-smelling rice.

'Fuck! Fuck! Fuck!' Ronan repeats after me as he zooms out of the kitchen like a tornado. I hold my head for a moment and try to gather my bearings…and the biryani.

'Just sweep it back into the casserole and serve it,' hisses the Thought Bubble connivingly. I am tempted to give it a thought, but then decide against it. It doesn't seem right.

On the other hand, what could possibly go wrong? It's not like it fell into a gutter or something. The kitchen floor was swept and mopped this very morning. And I don't have any other food lying around in the house. Tell you what, I'll just heat it for a few extra minutes in the microwave—that should fix all the germs. Anyway, this biryani is wayyy cleaner than Ronan's grubby hands that seem to leave sticky, greasy stains on everything he lays them on.

I gingerly collect the rice into the vessel and head out to put it on the table.

'Fuck! Fuck! Fuck!' Ronan is still chanting as he runs around in circles with a toy plane in his hands.

'Shut up, Ronan!' I glare at him. What if Jacinta hears him saying that? I would be done for… Uh oh, too late. She's already standing at the doorway, looking livid.

'Who taught him that? And you can't ask my boy to shut up!' she asks in a tight voice and I can practically feel myself crumble.

'I'm sorry. It just slipped out of my mouth and he caught onto it, I guess,' I offer apologetically. Why are three-year-olds such horrible people? I mean, couldn't he have waited to say that when his mom was away!

'Come here, Ronan,' she says sharply. 'And don't utter that word ever again. Well-bred people don't use that kind of language.'

Well-bred people! OK, I see it. That was below the belt, but seriously, what world is she living in? I'm sure the Queen of England herself must have used the F-word at least a few times in her life. The prude! I'll give her a piece of my well-bred mind right now if that's what she wants...

'Calm down, Kairavi,' whispers the Thought Bubble. 'This is not the time.'

I ritualistically draw in five deep breaths and to my surprise, the urge to punch Jacinta in the face recedes... somewhat. She is reaching out for the biryani and is about to stuff Ronan's face with it.

'Jacinta! Don't eat that!' I shout almost impulsively.

She turns to looks at me with a furrowed brow. 'Now what?'

'I... I think it doesn't smell too good. Let's all go out for lunch. There's a nice restaurant just around the corner,' I stammer.

Jacinta picks up the bowl and gives it a long, hard sniff. 'Smells perfect to me.'

'No...no...it's not good. Trust me. Let's just go out. Please.' I realize I'm practically begging at this stage.

Jacinta shrugs and leaves her chair, and I let out a sigh of relief.

The lunch at Candies goes rather peacefully, without any backhanded comments and jibes from Jacinta. Oh, I know what I'll call her—Jacinta the Jiber, or Jacky the Jiber. Ha! That sounds funny. Jacky the Jiber. A small giggle escapes my lips.

'What are you laughing at?' she asks.

'Me? No, nothing... I'm just happy to have you here!' I say brightly, but she just rolls her eyes. At least now if she catches diarrhea, it won't be my fault.

I try to make small talk when we get back home, but she just keeps responding in monosyllables. I'm prepared to do all the talking, but I'd really appreciate it if Jacinta would at least look me in the face when I'm talking to her. She just goes about her business, casting judgment-filled glances at everything in my house and treating me like a personal butler. Little wonder that her husband left her for another woman...

'Hey hey! That's a bit uncalled for, isn't it!' intervenes the Thought Bubble, making me feel terribly guilty about having such unnecessarily mean thoughts. All that stress seems to be messing with my head...

Four

I've never felt so happy and relieved to see Vivian. I mean I feel happy every time I see him, but this is on a whole other level. I wrap my arms tightly around him as soon as he comes in. He must have sensed my nervousness because he runs his disinfectant-smelling hands along my face.

'All OK?' he whispers slightly in my ear. I nod unsurely and he rubs my back, as if to say, 'Kudos, brave girl!'

Vivian's eyes light up as soon as he sees Ronan and the little tornado runs straight into his arms. I am really amazed at how much this guy can run in a single day. Honestly, if I could run even a small fraction of that, I would be size sub-zero in no time!

Jacinta and Vivian can barely exchange a hug because

Ronan has practically hijacked the whole scene. He is perched on Vivian's lap and is telling him some bizarre imaginary stories involving spiders and blood. Jacinta smiles for the first time since morning. I just hope she doesn't tell Vivian about the F-word I taught Ronan. I even tried teaching the brat a little song in the afternoon, to kind of make up for it, but the tyke didn't catch one single word of it.

As I watch the three of them huddled up on a sofa, I realize that for the first time in months, this house has a family-family vibe. I mean Vivian and I hang out here all the time, but it is not quite the same thing as having everyone together. The laughter. The noise.

The initial frenzy of seeing each other after months soon wanes and we all settle together in the living room with our respective drinks. I'm glad I stocked up on some tetra packs of juice, so even Ronan is not left out.

'So, you guys not planning to live-in or something?' asks Jacinta abruptly, shifting her gaze between Vivian and me. I know what she's trying to do here, so I choose not to answer that question at all.

'We will, Jackie. When the time is right,' answers Vivian confidently. 'We have our whole lives to live-in together, right, Kay?' He looks at me and gives me a knowing smile that just warms me up inside.

'I know! You must need your space too, once in a while?' says Jacinta with a smile.

Space? What does she mean? Why would Vivian need space from me?

'No, Jackie. I would never need space from Kay. It's just that...it's her parents' house and I just don't feel right living here like a freeloader. More a question of ethics, you see?' he explains coolly.

Really. Is that it? Is that why he refused to move in with me all these months? He never put it that way before. This is news to me. I mean, I know Vivian is a little, umm... traditional about certain things, such as marriage, but I never thought this was that big an issue with him.

I wouldn't mind him being the 'freeloader', as he puts it. Only if he'd ask me. For now, I'm just glad he's fielding all these pesky questions from Jacinta (which I bet she's asking just to tick me off) and he's doing a pretty awesome job of it.

Overall, it is going well, better that expected even. Jacinta looks quite happy. 'Beautiful watch, Kay,' Jacinta comments as she peers over to look at the silver Tag Heuer straddling my wrist. I can't believe she's actually saying something good about me, even if it is about my watch!

'Thanks! It was a gift from Viv...on our first anniversary,' I say proudly. I can't help but blush a little as the memories of that very special day flash in my mind. I had only briefly gasped at the watch at a mall and a week later, it was on my bedside, wrapped in shiny blue paper.

'Of course, it must be... It looks expensive.'

Wait...*What! Does she think I can't buy a watch on my own? That I am a gold-digger or something?* My ears are growing hot with anger and I shoot a look at Vivian, who looks relatively unperturbed.

'Yeah it was,' retorts Vivian coolly. 'In fact it is such a funny coincidence...we bought each other his and her versions of the same style...cheesy, right?' he says waving his fist to show off his Tag Heuer as he winks at me. I suppress a chortle. This is why I love him so much. Of course, I didn't get him that watch...

'Gimme...this mine,' butts in Ronan as he climbs over me to tug at the watch around my wrist.

'Umm, baby...why don't you play with your cars right here?' I say awkwardly, not quite wanting to hand over my precious gift to the crummy hands of a three-year-old. But he keeps tugging while looking up at me with large puppy-dog eyes. *How do these kids manage to do that—this puppy-eyed thing? It's crazy!*

'I'll get you a nice watch just like this after you've had dinner, OK, Ronan?' I say sweetly. See, even I can be smart and tactful.

'But I want now!' His voice is now a pitch higher and something tells me this is going to turn ugly.

'Just give it to him for a few minutes. We don't want tantrums to spoil the evening, do we?' suggests Jacinta with a smile. *Easy for her to say!*

Reluctantly, I peel off the watch and hand it over to the tyke...but not before shooting him a wait-till-we-are-alone kind of look. It is another matter that he totally ignores it. His eyes are gleefully fixated on the shiny new toy. What's with these new-age kids anyway? Why can't they just do the crossword puzzles on the disposable table mats like everyone else?

But I must admit, it does rein him in for a while. We are able to have a conversation for ten minutes straight without him whining about something or the other, which is a huge achievement. Trust me.

Vivian and I are listening attentively as Jacinta gushes about this big coup with a media house that her company has just landed. Frankly, I'm just trying to look barely interested without rolling my eyes too obviously...

I'm trying hard to smile and pace my nods appropriately, and maybe even drop a 'wow' or two at regular intervals when I hear a loud 'glug' from below. I look down to find something sink to the bottom of my giant Sangria glass. For a moment, I think it must be a lizard, but the clink of metal against glass is unmistakable.

'Nooooooo!' I scream and plunge my arm in to fish it out. But the damage has been done. I can't hear it ticking anymore. It is dead. My Tag Heuer is dead. Memories of our first anniversary...our love...dead. Gone to a red, bloody grave.

Ronan has been mildly scolded by his mother and is now crying at the top of his lungs. Honestly, I think he deserves more than a scolding. He should be quarantined in a stinky bathroom or something. I can feel hot tears welling up in my eyes.

'It's alright, Kay…it's waterproof,' comes Vivian's reassuring voice as he gently squeezes my thigh. Waterproof. Yes of course. I breathe a sigh of relief. How could I forget? I fuckin' scuba-dived in this thing once. But I'm still pissed at Ronan. What if it was not waterproof?

'Control, Kay, don't lose it now,' reminds the Thought Bubble.

'It's OK, Ronan…happens to the best of us,' I say with the fakest, sweetest smile I can proffer when all I want to do is twist his ear until it burns like lava.

But I can tell that he's already over the whole thing. He is grinning and running around in circles with a bowl of popcorn, which is just waiting to spill over to the ground. Frankly, I've just given up—I'll just clean the house at one go once these guys leave. No point struggling in between.

In due course of time, the popcorn does spill and Ronan says, 'Fuck! Fuck! Fuck!' really loud.

I go red with mortification. Jacinta gives me an accusatory stare and Vivian is trying to make sense of what just happened. It doesn't take him long to put two and two together. Oh God, I know I've messed up, but I don't want

Vivian to be angry. Jacinta already thinks I'm a crass woman who knows nothing better than to teach dirty words to kids who can barely talk.

To my surprise, Vivian just laughs it off. I don't understand why, but he's somehow amused at the idea of his three-year-old nephew flinging cuss words all over the place.

'It's not funny, Viv,' says Jacinta sternly.

'Yeah, no...but the way he says it is so cute,' replies Vivian between chortles.

Phew! At least he's not pissed at me.

At night when we are by ourselves, I even apologize to Vivian about corrupting his nephew.

'I always wanted to be the one to teach him nasty things, but I'm glad you did it for me...and thanks for being so understanding around Jacinta... I know she can be pretty tough to deal with sometimes...' he says with the crinkliest smile as we both snuggle closer.

Yeah, I'm not exactly going to contest that! 'She hates me, doesn't she?' I squeak in a low voice that makes me sound like a little school girl.

'No, she doesn't hate you at all! She's just a little...well, unaccepting of people in the beginning. No one can hate you, Kay...at least not for long.'

The house is unusually quiet in the morning. I see Jacinta making coffee, but the little monster is nowhere to be seen, although he is usually the first to wake up every morning.

'Ronan not up yet?' I ask.

'No, he's down with fever. Didn't sleep well last night,' says Jacinta morosely.

I can see the bags under her eyes and I kinda feel bad for her and Ronan. Sure, he is a devil incarnate, but I don't want him to have fever or anything. I quietly sneak up to his bed and touch his forehead. It is slightly warm and he is squirming.

'Sleep, sleep,' I say softly, running a hand through his hair. For the first time, I notice they are just like Vivian's.

'Kay, hold me,' he whispers in a croaky voice and I can tell his nose is blocked. Poor thing. I snuggle into the sheets beside him and collect him in my arms. He is so tiny and warm. And he actually looks cute when he's not doing all those evil things.

'I thought you didn't like me,' I say without even thinking.

'I like Kay,' he replies defiantly as if I've figured him all wrong.

I pull him close and we just lie quietly for some time until he drifts back to sleep again.

Five

'*W*hat! You are going to the Maldives next week? What for?' I squeak as Vivian gently breaks the news to me. Well, there ought to be nothing perturbing about that piece of information. Vivian travels for work pretty often, except that his birthday is in ten days and I have been hoping to make it awesome for him.

'Relax. It's only for a week!' he says gently as he pulls me into his broad chest and plants a kiss on my forehead.

'But...but...your birthday...'

'Oh come on now, Kay. It's just a birthday. And we'll celebrate it when I get back.'

Sure, I could do all of that another day, but it wouldn't quite be the same, would it?

'Now please don't make that sad kitty face,' he says, breaking me out of my reverie. I nod half-heartedly. He just doesn't get it, does he? Sometimes I wish he wasn't so practical about everything.

'Want to go out for dinner... Italian?'

My eyes light up ever so slightly. We hardly get to have dinner dates these days and some lasagna would definitely be comforting.

The waiter places a plate of cheesy, saucy wonder on the table, but surprisingly, it can't get my mind off the whole Maldives thing. I don't know why it is making me so miserable. Probably because of all the buildup to the occasion I have created in my mind? I silently dig my fork into the dish and start fiddling around with the layers.

'What's wrong, Kay? You not hungry?' Vivian knows how much I love lasagna and of late I'd even been pestering him to bring me here.

'Can I come with you?' The words flow out of my mouth before I can even register them in my thoughts. It must have caught Vivian off guard just as it does me, because he just sits silently for a couple of minutes as I look at him expectantly.

'Kay, sweetheart, it's an orthopedic conference,' he starts

patiently. 'I'm going to be busy all day with presentations and workshops...'

'But you'll be free in the evenings, no?' I press on. The idea of accompanying him to the Maldives has begun to take over my mind...and all logic.

Vivian lets out a loud sigh and sinks back into his seat. A moment later, he leans forward and takes both my hands in his, from across the table.

'Kay. The organizers are paying only for my tickets and stay. It's going to cost us a bomb if you come along. We have to save up for our future, haven't we? There is so much we have to do together. And it's just a birthday...no biggie!'

His honey-coloured eyes soften as he looks into mine and squeezes my palms. Wait, did he just say 'future'?

'Future? What future?' I grumble. 'It's not like we are married or anything.'

'Don't!' hisses the Thought Bubble. 'You promised not to bring up the "M" word!'

Oh well, too late now. I can't contain that sudden pang of annoyance. He hasn't even proposed the 'M' word and here he is, planning home loans and college funds for kids that are nowhere on the horizon. I half expect him to freak out because I have broken the pact, but to my surprise, he just keeps calm and smiles.

'But we will get married eventually, won't we? I'm just waiting for some funds to come in and this conference is a great opportunity. I don't want to spend my entire life in this pathetic job and you know it.'

Yes, yes I do. He wants to have his own practice...blah...

'Now cheer up, will you? Tiramisu?' Vivian knows how to press all the right buttons when I'm upset. These guys make the most perfect tiramisu in all of Mumbai.

'Watch the carbs, lady,' chides the Thought Bubble. OK, so I had to switch over to a new jeans size this month, but it's not like I eat tiramisu every day. Plus, Vivian is going away for a week, and that too on his birthday... I need something to make me feel good...instantly. And it's only this one time. I'm gonna hit the gym from Monday anyway. It's just one tiramisu...

The next morning, I wake up with an epiphany of sorts. *I am going to the Maldives to surprise Vivian on his birthday.*

Last year, I had baked him a red velvet cake that just, well, collapsed into itself...kind of like roads do in Mumbai during the monsoon. But don't ask me how that happened. I followed the recipe to the T and all that. I may not be a Nigella Lawson in the kitchen, but so what? I can still plan a birthday thingy for the man I love...and order the cake from someplace else.

Oh yes. Here's a fantastic idea right here—he's going to

be 33, so I'm going to surprise him with 33 gifts.

'Eww, isn't that cliché in a very teenagery sort of way?' cackles the Thought Bubble and I immediately dump the idea.

Teenagerey, heh? I remember I had done that for Baani once, when we were in college. I made her a little birthday basket with twenty-odd things—scarves, trinkets, makeup, a small purse, you know, the works...and it got her so thrilled. Gosh, that does seem a long time ago. How about a perfume? He uses perfumes all the time...even on regular days—as opposed to me, who uses them only on special occasions. But that would be so regular...and boring.

I decide I'm not going to buy stuff off the shops because you know, they can be so impersonal. I really want to give him something that I made...something he can have forever and maybe even show it to our children and grandchildren—if we ever get to that point. I've actually been painting a T-shirt secretly...a golden guitar on a black tee coz I know how much he loves rock 'n' roll. I swear he's going to jump at the sight of it. It looks gorgeous, even if I say so myself. And I even embroidered his initials on a hand-woven silk tie from Fabindia. I wasn't sure if I would be able to pull that off, but YouTube makes everything a cinch. This time around, it's all going to be perfect. And so romantic. I can already see it happening. I'll pop into his room as soon as the clock strikes twelve, just before the concierge brings in the bottle of champagne with a little love note and of course, the cake. But you know, the real birthday gift will be me. When the concierge is gone, we'll do some naughty stuff with the cake—we obviously can't eat all of it—and then sit under the stars on the beach and have a cozy little party of our own. The next day, I could book us for a couple's massage at the Veli Spa, and then plan a very special barbeque just for the two of us in the evening. And rope in a violin guy too if he's not too expensive. Yes, this is exactly what our relationship needs right now...some rekindling, and the Maldives would be the perfect place to start. Oh God, why didn't I think of all this before!

So the plan is all set, except for a teensy little problem—I don't have the money. You see, I'm not on a regular salary anymore, not that my previous one would have sufficed anyway. I check all my bank accounts and fixed deposits to see if I can go through with this and realize that if I do, I will go absolutely bankrupt and have a sizeable credit card bill to boot. Definitely not a smart thing to do.

Of course I could borrow from Mom and Dad, but somehow I don't like that idea anymore. I'm an independent girl and it's not like this is an emergency. It's just...a whim. A crazy whim. One that I can't seem to get over.

I pace up and down the living room, hoping for another epiphany to strike. Maybe I have a wad of cash stashed away somewhere? Maybe I have a secret savings account that I have forgotten about? Some useless jewelry that I can pawn off? Anything I can sell? Nope, nothing. Why do these resorts have to be so friggin' expensive? And on some godforsaken island?

How I wish right now that I'd been better with savings. Baani always nudged me to go easy on the shopping. If only I'd listened to her then, I'd probably have enough money to afford this trip. With that thought I find myself standing at the door to Baani's old room and in seconds, my face lights up with joy. There it is…there's my answer!

Moments later, I find myself creating an ad on a classified website titled 'Room for rent in Bandra East—females only'. To my luck, my phone starts tinkling minutes after. It is a girl looking to rent a room. I rub my palms in glee and ask her to come over and check out the apartment. This is what I love about Mumbai…there's always someone looking for a place to shack up.

She comes over the same evening. A wiry-looking girl of about 20, with wiry black hair and wiry arms. She's just so… wiry. Anyway. None of my business. She could be a walking-talking electric pole for fuck's sake and I couldn't care less, as long as she could pay. I just need the money…really quickly.

'Hi!' I smile brightly at her and proffer a hand. Got to look amicable.

'Hello,' she says nervously as her eyes scan the house.

'Come, let me show you the room,' I say, ushering her

in. I have spent some time cleaning up and I've even sprayed some lemongrass oil like they do in expensive hotels because I really want to seal the deal as quickly as possible.

'New to Mumbai?' I ask casually, trying to make small talk.

'Yes, I just joined National College. Was staying with a relative, but can't stay there forever, you know.'

'Ya, I totally get it,' I concur. College student huh? This is just perfect, because I'm not getting into any of those legal thingies. It takes too long and come on, who has the time to go to courts to sign papers, etc.

Moreover, if I have to keep a tenant—legally that is—Mom and Dad will have to come in to complete the formalities. I think I did the smart thing by not telling them at all! I'll just tell everyone else that she's a friend...or a cousin...or something. I mean in Mumbai who even cares... there are old people dying in their crummy little apartments all the time only to be discovered when their flesh starts to rot. I'm sure it will never come to that.

'How much is the rent?' she asks after scrutinizing every inch of the room.

Oh well, I haven't thought of what to quote. I don't even know what the rents are like in this area. Shit! I should have done my research. OK, no need to panic. I'll just quote a realistic figure; she's a college student, so...

'₹20,000,' I blurt out.

'I'll take it,' she says almost immediately. *Shit, did I quote too low? She didn't even try to haggle...*

'But...but you will need to pay six month's rent in advance...you know, as security deposit,' I say hesitatingly. I'm just shooting arrows in the air hoping against hope that they'll hit the target. I have absolutely no idea how this thing works.

What if she asks me some legal questions? Or something about real estate? Oh dear, why am I so terrible at this?!

'Cool. I'll ask Dad to deposit a cheque in your account by tomorrow,' she smiles. 'I'll get my stuff tomorrow morning, if that's OK?'

'O...of course!' I stammer. That's it? It's done? So quickly? I hope I've done the right thing. I gulp in anticipation. My hands are trembling the way they do every time I do something on the sly without telling Mom and Dad.

'Oh come on...it's not against the law, is it?' urges the Thought Bubble.

Of course. Of course it is not against the law. Baani lived with me all these years. But somehow, I can't seem to shake away that nagging feeling. Have I done the right thing? I mean, what could possibly go wrong?

I think of calling Vivian to take his advice, but I know he'll just flip. He takes all this legal paperwork way too seriously, like everything else. He's no fun when it comes to breaking rules. And what am I going to tell him? That I need the money to surprise him in the Maldives? That would just defeat the entire purpose, wouldn't it?

I immediately pick up the phone and dial Baani.

'You what?!' Baani screeches as I tell her of my plans.

'Relax, I have it all sorted,' I assure her.

'But no background check, nothing? Are you really going to share your house with a complete stranger, Kay? And what if you don't get along? What if she runs away with all your stuff? What if she is a serial killer on the prowl? When will you stop being crazy?'

I burst out laughing. So typical of Baani to get all worked up over nothing. She does that all the time.

'Baani, she's just a college student. And if things don't work out, I'll ask her to vacate the room. Simple as that!'

'OK, if you say so....' she says in a low voice.

Even over the phone, I can sense that Baani is not too happy with my decision. But that's Baani for you—always worrying about me and always looking out for me. I love her to bits.

But the coolest thing is that tomorrow, I'll have the monies...and I'll book the tickets. Maldives, here I come!

Six

*I*t's been a couple of days since Farah, my new flatmate, moved in, and from what I have sensed, she's quite aloof and likes to keep to herself. Which is perfectly fine by me. I mean, I don't need a friend. I just need the money. And both of us know that this is a very temporary arrangement, so no point getting too pally and bonding too much.

I'm leaning over the kitchen counter waiting for the butter to heat up so that I can pour in the beaten eggs when Farah strides into the kitchen. She is wearing neon-pink yoga pants and a matching spaghetti top, looking all bright and fresh. I look at my own grey track pants and worn-out vest and feel a pang of embarrassment.

'Been out somewhere?' I casually ask.

'Yeah, just exercising in the park,' she says with a tight smile as she reaches for a bottle of water.

'Nice. Want me to make you some eggs?' I ask.

'No, thanks. I don't eat eggs,' she says and proceeds to pull out a bundle of spinach from the fridge. She pops it into the blender with some soymilk, whizzes it for a minute, pours it into a mug and chugs it down at once.

'Eww! Did she just do that?!' says a very disgusted Thought Bubble and I'm feeling a little nauseous at the sight. Also a little resentful.

'You probably shouldn't be having that,' she comments as I begin to grate some cheddar onto my omelet. I look up to her in horror. If there is one thing I hate more than wiry people drinking spinach smoothies in my kitchen, it is wiry people telling me I'm too fat to add cheese to my omelet.

'My dietician says I should have a protein-rich breakfast and cheese is all protein,' I say defensively as I flip my omelet so the cheese sizzles audibly. I plonk it onto my plate and butter my toast extra nicely, as if to prove a point, and march across to my room to have my breakfast in peace without any patronizing eyes judging me.

God, how I miss those days when Baani and I cooked awesome stuff and ate at the dining table, chatting for hours. There will never be another flatmate like Baani. And as for Farah, I have already decided that I don't like her.

Actually, I hate her. How dare she! The...the...bitch!

I am just about to head to bed when Farah emerges from her room wearing the shortest, crappiest-looking red skirt and a strappy silver top—also crappy looking. And you should have seen her makeup...it was so loud, almost cacophonic. I mean, who on earth does smokey eyes and red lips together?

'Tch tch...poor little small town girl. Too desperate to fit in,' whispers the Thought Bubble. She kinda looks slutty in a clownish sort of way, or clownish in a very slutty sort of way. Oh whatever! She could definitely use some sartorial support and I would have been happy to lend her some, only if she asked for it first. But on second thoughts, let her go out and get laughed at, I think to myself, remembering the cheese-on-omelet incident. She is already so patronizing to me.

But something inside me cannot hold back. 'Umm, Farah...I think your makeup is looking a little...err...dark. Or maybe it is the lights, I don't know,' I offer cautiously, careful not to sound too critical. She might be a freak, but I really don't want a young girl like her to become a target of ridicule in this big evil city. And college kids can be pretty mean at times... I clearly remember how they treated Baani when she was new in college, calling her the nastiest of names.

Farah doesn't respond, but she takes a moment to inspect her face from all angles in the small wrought iron-framed mirror right next to the door. Baani had put it there because she always liked to check herself out before leaving the house. 'This is what's in right now,' she says flatly, in a very you-went-to-college-a-decade-ago sort of way.

'Fine,' I say with a cool shrug. Let her get laughed at. She probably deserves it.

'I'll just fix it,' she says with a smile and disappears into the room. When she comes out, she looks a lot better. The lips are a peachy nude instead of scarlet and she's even thrown on a shrug to balance the attire.

I sigh warmly and tuck myself into bed. Vivian is travelling tomorrow and I just have to hold up my excitement for a few more hours. Yesterday, when I was at his place helping him pack his bags, I almost gave away everything when I offered to bring over anything he might forget to pack in. Thankfully, he took it as a lame joke and laughed out loud.

Seven

I try to fake a sad face as I drop Vivian off at the airport, but I'm so full of glee inside. I've booked myself on a flight tomorrow, so that I can reach there just in time for Vivian's birthday, which is day after. In fact, right after I get out of here, I'm going to do a bit of shopping for him and maybe visit the salon for a slight touch-up...because we are going to be holidaying in the Maldives!

Oh God, there is so much to do and so little time! I have to get my facial and waxing done right away. I'll even get a body polish done, so that my skin looks all smooth and yummy on the beach. I'm going to floor him. Maybe I'll even get new highlights in my hair.

'For the last time: It. Is. Not. Your. Honeymoon!' butts in

the Thought Bubble, splashing cold water over all my sex-on-the-beach fantasies. OK, maybe I'm going a little overboard, but a basic grooming session is perfectly in order.

I stride into my favourite salon on Linking Road, where Roma, my beautician, is already waiting for me because I had booked an appointment.

'Looks like I'm going to be here for a while,' I say with a smile. I just love being in a salon. It is so relaxing.

I exhale deeply and settle down into the massage chair. 'Any special occasion, madam?' Roma inquires, looking at the smug smile plastered on my face.

I've been hoping someone would ask me! 'Actually, I'm going to the Maldives tomorrow, to surprise my boyfriend,' I say enthusiastically.

'Oh wow!' She is clearly impressed. I mean who wouldn't be, right?

'Then you should probably get the Special Facial, since it is going to be a special occasion,' she winks at me cheekily. So it's not just me. Everyone else thinks of sex on the beach when they hear 'Maldives'.

'Yeah…yeah…why not!' I retort, wondering why I hadn't thought of that myself. I always get the regular Fruit Cleanup, not because it is the cheapest one on the service menu, but because it suits my skin. So much so that I haven't even felt the need to try out anything new. But now that I have fallen into a small fortune, what with the rental deposit and all, I can surely afford a few indulgences for myself. And the tickets and resort bookings have been taken care of anyway...

'Try the Diamond Facial, it gives great results,' she chirps as I scan the service menu, mulling over my options.

The Diamond Facial is four grand. I gulp slightly, but then an image of my face glittering like diamonds against the turquoise waters of the Maldives flashes before me. Oh what the heck! It's not every day that you go all the way to the Maldives to surprise your boyfriend on his birthday, do you?

I reply in the affirmative and fish out my Kindle from my handbag while she begins to heat the wax.

'How about a bikini wax, madam? Since you are going to the Maldives?' I look up at her, and her face has the same cheeky grin. It's almost as if she's more excited than me about this whole adventure.

'No, thanks,' I say, slightly repulsed at the idea.

'It feels really soft and smooth and like butter after that,' she chides on.

I look up at her. I've never tried waxing the 'it' in question. Trimming, sure, but ripping out hair from the roots—God, no!

But she seems really confident—surely she knows what she's talking about. And there always is a first time for everything, isn't there? And what if the 'it' really ends up buttery smooth—now that would be some birthday surprise, wouldn't it?! Ahem...

I weigh my options for a moment and am about to chicken out because frankly, the thought of some stranger ripping hair off my crotch is making me shudder.

'We do about twenty of these every day and most women get it done every month,' she adds as though she is reading my mind, and in the process making me feel like some moron for missing the bus, when everyone else clearly seems to be enjoying the ride. Why else would they come for it again?

So before I know it, I am lying spread-eagled on a very narrow bed. Roma senses my anxiety, and makes random chit-chat just to make me feel comfortable. It doesn't make me feel any better, knowing that she is standing between my legs and my hoo-haa is laid on full display right in front of her. *Thank God I showered before coming here.*

I flinch a little as she begins to prune my lady garden, and then proceeds to spoon the hot, sticky wax all over it. She's so cool about it all. I wonder if she probably spends all her day clearing bushes between legs, which she probably does.

'It won't take long, I promise,' she says with a reassuring smile.

I nod nervously.

'You've been getting your hands and legs waxed all your life. How bad can it be?' urges the Thought Bubble. Yeah, I'm probably exaggerating. Many people have a really low threshold for pain, but not me. I have two tattoos and I braved my way through both of them. Surely, this can't be more painful than a tattoo...

'OWWWWWWW...' I shriek as Roma pulls away the strip. Tears blur my vision and I swear I could die. My head feels heavy and light at the same time.

'What the hell?!' I snap at Roma, who looks triumphantly at the patch of hair on the strip.

'I'm sorry, ma'am...but the growth is thick and it's your first time, so...'

She's no longer compassionate and assuring. She's very matter-of-fact. Almost brutal. Like she snared me into this. Like she derives some strange sadistic pleasure out of doing this to unsuspecting subjects. All the salon girls will probably giggle over the nasty details after I'm gone.

That's it. I'm going to abandon Mission Buttery Smooth. There are a million other ways to look sexually attractive, but you can only try them out if you are alive.

'No, Roma...no more...' I say, shaking my head vehemently from side to side.

'But...you can't...'

'Of course, I can!' I say as I get up from the bed and bend over to look at my precious jewel box. It is throbbing with pain...and...and it looks like a spiky, patchy crimson mess!

I moan and throw myself back onto the bed, spreading my legs wide apart, voluntarily this time. Roma is visibly pleased and she quickly rushes in to finish the job, lest I change my mind.

The next half an hour can at best be described as the worst minutes of my entire existence as Roma ladles hot wax over my already sore skin and violently pulls at the strips to 'get it done as quickly as possible'. Noble sentiment, except that it makes me want to kill myself...or her. Mostly her.

'AAAHHHHHHHHHHH!!!' I scream as the last bit of 'growth' is pulled out, and as usual, Roma ignores my helpless cries. My mouth is dry from all the yelling and screaming, but somewhere along the way, I had stuffed a kerchief into my mouth (Roma's idea) to stay civilized. Also, because the other staff members kept knocking on the chamber door and asking if everything was alright. Of course everything is not alright!

The agony lasts for what seems like forever, and by the end of it, I am bleary eyed, half-dead and panting. I realize I can't even walk straight as I hobble out of the torture chamber. Roma suggests that I take a painkiller or something. Sure, I will.

At least my face will glitter like diamonds even if my lady parts look like uncut rubies.

I limp my way to the apartment and find Farah sprawled in front of the TV in the living room. Great, just what I needed! I purposefully ignore her and make my way to the room.

'Shit! What happened to your face?' she exclaims and my hand instinctively flies up to my cheek. It certainly doesn't feel smooth like it did after the facial. I rush over to the mirror.

'AAARRRGH!' There are nasty red blotches all over and it is going to break out. I just know it. Damn the Diamond Facial! What did it have, real diamonds?! On an ordinary day, this wouldn't have bothered me much, but I have to go to the Maldives tomorrow. The whole of my nether region has been rendered useless, and now my face too! Oh God, what have I done to deserve this?! I break down in tears.

My first impulse is to call up Mom and howl on the phone. She gets worried, yes, but she doesn't miss an opportunity to reprimand me for 'trying out stupid things' despite knowing that 'I have sensitive skin'. But in the end, she does advise me to rub some aloe vera gel to bring down the inflammation.

'Here, eat this,' Farah thrusts a tiny white pill before me. I bet she's trying to poison me. I know she never liked me anyway. Am I looking so ugly that she wants me dead?

'Take it. It's an anti-allergic. It will help, trust me,' she says not-too-warmly. I gingerly take the pill and gulp it down with water. Better dead than ugly.

It has been half an hour since I took the pill, but my face is still red and blotchy. It's even begun to sting a little now. But I'm feeling drowsy. I knew Farah was up to no good... she's poisoned me. What if Baani was right? What if Farah ran away with all my stuff? I really don't give a damn. I have to sleep.

Eight

Shit! For how long have I been sleeping? I have an effin' flight to catch! I stumble out of bed and hurriedly make my way to the bathroom. A smile spreads across my face as I look into the mirror—the red patches have disappeared and my skin looks close to normal again. I rush out to thank Farah for whatever it was that she fed me, only to find that she's already left for the day. I write her a 'Thanks!' on a Post-it note and stick it on the fridge so she'll see it in the evening. I've even decided to get her something from the Maldives because she helped me save face...quite literally. Also, my crotch is no longer on fire—hallelujah!

Soon, I find myself queuing up to check-in the baggage. There is a sudden deluge of red bangles everywhere. It is the honeymooners. I feel kinda awkward and out of place to be the sad single lady. I, apart from a couple of locals, are the only ones on the flight not on a honeymoon. Well, I may not be on a literal honeymoon...but Viv and I are going to be together and stuff. So for all practical purposes...it is a honeymoon, isn't it? A prenuptial honeymoon.

In all my excitement, I scuffle out of the plane and make way for the baggage. I wouldn't have had to check-in the bags if only I had stuck to my packing list. I always pack light...but this time around, I got a little carried away. I'm going to need all that stuff anyway. I obviously can't be wearing the same swimming suit all the time. And then I'll need something flowy for the day and something fancy for the evening. I even packed in a maxi dress that was in the resort-wear section of my favourite shopping website. And true to its tag, it really can't be worn anyplace other than a resort. So it had to come along. And I kept my purple stilettos with spiked heels, just in case.

As our tiny plane lands on an even tinier airstrip, I take in a moment to soak in the beautiful aerial view of the archipelagos. To be honest, I have never seen water so blue, even though I have lived by the sea practically all my life.

Once again, I seem to be the only one by the conveyor belt without my arms swathed in bangles. The honeymooners are either holding onto each other tightly or smiling annoyingly into each other's eyes, depending on the level of PDA they are comfortable with, and I stand sourly in the corner waiting for my stuff, which is taking the longest time to arrive. The crowd is gradually waning, as is the quantity of luggage on the belt, and soon I'm the only one left standing. A knot forms in my stomach. Has my baggage not arrived? I frantically peer over the belt hoping for my little lime-green wonder to emerge from under the rubber flaps, but there is no sign of it. Vivian thinks the excruciating brightness of the suitcase makes it impossible to miss. I love the colour to bits, but yes, it is impossible to miss. Isn't that a perk? The conveyor belt wheezes past right under my nose and the bangle brigade has long since left. I make a mad dash for the help desk and demand to be told the whereabouts of my precious suitcase by the lady on the other side. She looks at me nonchalantly—as if losing one's luggage is a regular everyday thing. Sure it must be. I mean, I've heard stories, but I never thought it would happen to me. Not on this trip at least. I mean what am I supposed to do...roam around that posh resort in my tattered travelling jeans and this miserable grey T-shirt when everyone else will be...well...

'Your boarding pass please,' she says coolly. This clearly isn't a matter of worry for her.

I fumble through my handbag, which is no less deeper than a well by the way, and fish it out for her. She inspects it while dialling a number and mumbles something in a language I don't understand.

'Madam, we are sorry, but your bag got left behind in Kochi. It will arrive tomorrow by the next flight and we'll have it sent to your resort. Please leave your details here,' she says as she pushes a leather-bound book in my general direction.

'What do you mean it got left behind? How can a bag get left behind?!' I yelp helplessly knowing that this kind of shit happens. It is just one of the side effects of air travel.

'I'm extremely sorry, ma'am, but you'll have to wait till tomorrow.'

I can feel my hands tremble as I walk away from the desk. Here I was planning to change into my sexy white dress and Vivian's favourite lingerie and now I don't even have a change of undies! What the hell am I going to do? OK, OK, don't panic. There is absolutely no reason to panic. The luggage will arrive in less than 24 hours. Surely I can manage till then. Maybe I'll just buy some stuff here.

Grudgingly, I walk towards the resort's reception counter next to the airport exit, and before I can make up my mind about the shopping, I am promptly whisked off to a boat right outside the airport.

'Do you have any shops on the island?' I ask the concierge as he offers me a welcome drink and a chilled face towel that smells like lemongrass. These guys really know how to pamper their guests.

'Of course, madam…we have two boutiques right inside the resort.'

Boutiques! I heave a sigh of relief. It's not going to be all that terrible after all. I'll just buy something nice to get me by till tomorrow.

I gulp down my lemonade and sit out on the deck waiting in anticipation. I hope I don't run into Vivian today. I quickly pull out my scarf from the bag and wrap it around my face, and put on my enormous sunglasses for good measure. This way, even if I bump into him, he'll probably not be able to recognize me. Then I'll just quickly sneak my way to the room and camp there till midnight. Oh God, I just can't wait!

After checking in and briefing the manager on my plans, I slither into the boutique, my scarf and sunglasses stuck firmly in place. The shelves have only a few select items—all of them exquisite, though. I gingerly pick up a blue kaftan and place it against myself. This should do it. I flip over the price tag and for a moment, my heart loses its rhythm. It is 150 flippin' dollars! Back home in Mumbai, I could buy a kaftan like this off Fashion Street for less than 150 bucks. This birthday surprise has anyway put a humongous dent in my savings. I gulp and quickly put it back in its spot. I casually browse through some of the price tags and each is progressively more horrifying than the last. I guess the travel jeans and the frumpy grey T-shirt will have to do for now.

Deflated, I make my way to the room and plonk onto the bed. Even though it is the cheapest room in the resort, it is pretty awesome—in fact, better than any I have stayed in before. Vivian is in one of the beach-facing cottages, I reckon. These doctor guys have it so cool. Just because he is one of the presenters, he gets the entire trip sponsored by the pharmaceutical company. Anyway, I am going to move into his room tomorrow and I'll have a little stretch of beach all to myself...ourselves. I am still upset about the luggage, but what the heck, I can always give him the gifts later. Oh God, he'll be so thrilled to see me!

It is five minutes to midnight and I can feel my heart racing inside of me. I have the table all set up just outside his room, complete with the cake, champagne and all that jazz. The resort guys were extra nice to have put in some orchids and scented candles on their own for a nice touch. And it is a full moon night...yippee!

I tiptoe over to the back door, because I have the table set on the beach, and give it a gentle knock. What? Do I hear noises? Must be the TV. Of course it is the TV. Poor Viv. Fancy being alone on your birthday!

The door clicks open and there he is...my man! He spends a few speechless moments before lunging forward to give me the tightest hug. 'Kay...you crazy girl...how did you...?'

Before he can finish his sentence, I seal his mouth with a kiss.

'Happy birthday, sweetheart,' I squeal.

His face is beaming with joy—which is precisely what I wanted—and I can't stop grinning myself. But my smile shrinks into a dot when I look over his shoulder. There is Aisha...and five others in the room. 'Kairavi! How nice to see you here,' she says pleasantly and comes forward to hug me—one of those fake ones with air kisses and minimum body contact. My mood has completely changed and I'm alternating my gaze between Vivian and Aisha, trying to make sense of the situation. What the hell is she doing here!?

'OK, I think we'll leave you two lovebirds alone. Enjoy yourselves!' she chirps as she gestures to the others, and all of them make a beeline for the exit. I gaze after her suspiciously.

'Why is she here?' I ask sharply, turning to Vivian as soon as the door is shut behind us.

'She's one of the speakers in the conference,' Vivian says coolly and takes me into a hug. Yeah, that makes sense. She's an orthopedic surgeon too and she has all the reasons to be here in an orthopedic conference. But something doesn't quite feel right.

'What was she doing in *your* room?' I insist.

'Kairavi! All the doctors just came to wish me, that's all. Why are you getting so worked up?' His voice is soft and patient, and I feel like believing him. But I wonder if he knew she was going to be here?

'You're sounding like an over-possessive nag, you know that, right?' reminds the Thought Bubble and I quickly swallow the thousand questions I am about to hurl at Vivian. I came here to make his birthday special, not to interrogate him over some non-issue. And who is Aisha anyway? Vivian loves me, and only me. She can go bite my towel!

'Kay, I know what you are thinking. You have no reason to be worried. Aisha has changed and even apologized about what she did. She is really happy for us,' he says reassuringly, looking into my eyes.

I smile back at him. I love it when he's able to read my mind without me having to spell everything out. He knows me so well. Isn't that what true love is about?

And he's right. I'm getting worked up over nothing. We are all adults and we need to let go of the past. After all, it was all a year ago...

I'm not going to let Aisha spoil my mood. For all you know, she might actually be repenting. People change with time and maybe she's just accepted that she doesn't stand a chance with Vivian, despite her long legs, Barbie-like hair, lush Mesopotamian lips and annoyingly perfect lithe body.

'I smell something burningggg,' coughs the Thought Bubble and I realize I've allowed myself to be carried away by negative thoughts...again. *I mustn't*, I tell myself silently, and push Aisha out of my mind. She's not worth my time, not right now anyway, I decide.

'You made me a happy man today, Kay,' Vivian whispers into my ear and plants tender little kisses on my neck as we both fall into the springy bed. His lips have made their way onto mine and we both get entwined into a long, passionate kiss. His fingers creep up under my shirt and are just about to unhook my bra, when I stop him.

'Not now, Tiger,' I say mischievously and drag him out of bed.

'But why? Didn't you come all the way here to have steamy sex with me?' he teases.

'Yes, of course I did, but not before I give you a small birthday treat.' I blindfold him with a silk scarf.

'Ohhh...nice touch. Very kinky!' he says.

'Shut up, Vivian...we are not going to have sex right now!' I say with absolutely fake finality, unable to control my laughter. He's never like this in Mumbai. I take him by his hand and lead him out to the beach where everything is perfectly laid out, exactly like how I wanted.

I remove his blindfold and his face lights up like the million stars in the sky. *Oh God, I could live and die for this.* He grabs me and is just about to kiss me hard, when I discreetly point to the butler standing close by. Vivian frowns and loosens his grip reluctantly while I chuckle. I know he's super-conservative when it comes to PDA, and it can be a little annoying at times too (I mean holding hands in a mall isn't hurting anyone, right?), but today, I feel only love for him—in a way that I haven't felt in a long time. Maybe it's the moonlight or the waves glowing white, or the gentle salty breeze caressing our skins, or the starlit sky—everything feels out of this world...and so romantic.

I request our personal butler to leave as soon as we are served dinner so that we can be by ourselves and gaze tirelessly into each other's eyes. It's like falling in love all over again.

'Now can we please have some mind-blowing sex?' he asks as soon as the butler goes out of sight. I burst out laughing. It'd be cruel to say 'no' to the birthday boy.

I leave my chair to walk over to his side of the table, and plant myself in his lap, straddling him with my legs. The look in his eyes tells me that he wants me to take over. Fair enough, it's his birthday after all. I take his luscious lower lip between mine and nibble it ever so softly. Instinctively, his arms tighten around my waist and he draws me closer. Our breaths intermingle, as do our tongues, teasing and playing with each other, perfectly in sync. I just love the way his warm body feels pressed against mine. And God, that cologne! He knows what it does to me, which is why he makes it a point to wear it whenever we are together. After a while, we are too delirious to keep ourselves balanced on the chair anymore. Without exchanging a word or breaking the flow, we roll onto the soft white sand below us. His hand slides up my thigh, hitching the hem of my dress, as my body quivers in anticipation. Our kisses grow rougher and more urgent by the minute and I just can't wait for him to take me.

'I want you,' he whispers into my ear, once again reading my thoughts.

We make mad love through the night, panting, laughing, talking and just lying on the beach holding each other close and looking up at the starry skies. Life has never felt better. I'm so proud of myself...and so happy!

The next morning in the buffet area, as Vivian and I are sipping at our tropical fruit shakes, basking in the afterglow of the previous night, Aisha walks over to our table to say hi.

I respond with a tight, hesitant smile. 'I didn't want to disturb you two lovebirds,' she says extra sweetly.

'No, Aisha, that's alright,' says Vivian. 'Come sit with us.'

Why did he have to ask her to sit at our table? We were having such a good time by ourselves! Aisha makes a mildly apologetic face but sinks gracefully into the chair nevertheless. 'I hope you don't mind, Kairavi,' she says, squeezing my arm.

'No...no of course not,' I manage to stammer.

'Make her go away! And soon!' hisses the Thought Bubble, but I quickly muffle its voice. I'm going to look all confident and secure and unfazed by Aisha's presence, I decide resolutely.

'So how have you been, Aisha?' I ask with the sweetest smile I can manage, going a little overboard to hide my discomfort. I have to hold it together, I tell myself.

'Ah well, it's been a tough time, Kairavi,' she says, her voice suddenly low. 'My father...'

I throw a perplexed look at Vivian and he discreetly points a finger to the sky.

'I'm so sorry to hear that!' I say, feeling genuinely sad for Aisha. I'd met her father, Dr Dhawan, when I was admitted to the hospital in Goa (long story). He was grouchy but otherwise a fine man.

'What happened?'

'He had cancer,' butts in Vivian because Aisha has mascara-laced tears running down her cheeks. I rub her shoulders to comfort her, but instead, she leans onto Vivian's shoulder and breaks down into muffled sobs.

Vivian awkwardly places one arm around her and tries to console her while I watch helplessly. Something about the whole thing just doesn't feel right—my instincts say so.

I look at Vivian, who is being the good supportive friend, since they have been family friends for years, and I look at Aisha, who is snuggling deeper and deeper into his chest, while I am rendered totally irrelevant in the entire scene unfolding at that moment.

Then I catch her looking at me and smirking. *Okayyy... I get it. So this is what it is about! And to think that Aisha had turned over a new leaf! Hah, who was the bitch trying to fool?! Two can play this game. She may have won a battle, but she's going to sorely lose the bleedin' war. Vivian is mine and no long-legged witch is going to steal him away from me.* I feel hot and angry and I can feel blind rage surge up inside of me, but there is nothing I can really do right now that wouldn't make me look like a sore loser.

'Do you think Aisha still has feelings for you?' I ask Vivian as we lie in bed that night.

'No, she clearly said she didn't anymore,' he replies matter-of-factly. Why are men so naïve, taking every word at face value? Can't they see through the simplest of things?

'You asked her?'

'No! Are you crazy? She said so when she came up to me to apologize. She even has a boyfriend now,' he says confidently.

Oh Vivian, why are you such a simpleton? I shake my head inwardly, disappointed.

'Kay, her dad passed away just a couple of months ago. It's a hard time for her...maybe she's acting a little emotional, that's all.'

I nod my head reluctantly and snuggle closer, into his arms.

Aisha is going to be on my radar now, I decide. And I'm not going to let that creepy woman flit anywhere near Vivian, for as long as I can help it.

Nine

OK, so the first couple of days were very relaxing (and romantic), but now I am just about beginning to get a little pissed. Vivian is hardly around and all I do until lunch is lounge on the beach chair and be lazy with my e-reader. The fact that Aisha has such easy access to Vivian in the conference makes me even more miserable, but I draw solace from the fact that there will be fifty other people there, so there's hardly any chance of her indulging in any hanky-panky with my man.

I sit alone and spend my time gazing at all the beautiful people around. The guys and the girls, they are all so fit and toned, as if they were born into bikinis. Sometimes you can't help but hate these Europeans. I mean how come no one has a paunch or a love handle. It's bizarre! I very much wanted to flaunt my white-and-gold bikini but in the end, decided against it. Instead, I brought along a swimsuit that can be best described as...well, strategic. Of course, I depend on the sarong a lot. I have, however, promised to buy myself new beachwear when I am thin again.

'Yeah right! Like that's gonna happen,' says the Thought Bubble. Well, maybe not very soon, but I'll definitely get there. I've just read up on this amazing new diet in *Cosmo*. All the celebs are swearing by it. I'm going to get cracking on it as soon as I get to Mumbai, I resolve.

Luckily for me, Vivian returns early that evening. We take a long shower together and head out to the beach to watch the sunset. Vivian begins telling me about his presentations, but I shush him—who wants to hear about some boring orthopedic procedure when it's so beautiful and romantic around. I rush over to the beachside bar and grab a couple of cocktails for both of us. I know he's been working very hard, and he deserves some pampering.

Just as we both sit down to relax on our beach chairs, I see Aisha appearing from the other side of the beach. She's wearing a bright-orange bikini and I can almost feel my jaw slack. Her stomach is flat like a washboard, and I have never seen legs so shapely outside of a fashion magazine. The relaxation has fully waned and I am almost hyperventilating from anxiety.

'Vivian!' I squeak. 'Tell me about the presentation. Sorry I interrupted you earlier...' My voice is so wobbly and shrill that it's not even funny.

'It's boring stuff...let's just relax,' he says coolly as he pulls both his arms behind his head.

'OK...OK...just shield your eyes. I've heard the setting sun gives out a lot of infrared rays which can cause...err... cataract,' I retort, pulling his hat down over his eyes.

'Kairavi, just relax,' he says with an amused expression.

I look out from the corner of my eye and spot Aisha entering the water. *Yes, yes, go deep into the ocean where he can't see you.*

'Is something bothering you, love?'

Oh no no no. Telepathy is the very last thing I need right now.

'No!' I yelp. 'Let's...let's go inside. I'm... I'm feeling a little horny!'

Vivian bursts out in laughter and I smile at him sheepishly. I'm gonna do whatever it takes to save him from the clutches of this evil orange-bikini-donning diva, even if it makes me look like a deranged rabbit.

We are halfway to our room when we hear a scream.

'Help! Help!'

Shit. That's Aisha.

Vivian turns around and squints at the orange dot in the ocean. 'Is that Aisha?'

'Um no...must be someone else,' I reply. It's not like I want her to drown. Or maybe I do...

'I think I should go and check,' Vivian says as he takes off his T-shirt.

'Wait! You stay here, I'll go,' I offer on an impulse. I don't know how I came up with that, because I'm not even a good swimmer, but I also know that the water there is only waist-deep and Aisha is just playing one of her stupid games.

I take off my sarong and paddle into the water. Before she can say a word, I grab her by the hand and twist it behind her back, while at the same time nudging her towards the shore.

'It'll save you a lot of embarrassment if you just give up,' I hiss into her ear.

From the distance, I can see Vivian peering over anxiously. She doesn't say anything, but just jerks herself away from me and walks towards the shore, a sour expression on her face. She looks visibly miffed, and I can't stop myself from grinning like a triumphant idiot.

'Aisha! Are you alright?' Vivian rushes towards us as we both pull ourselves away from the water.

Is he not going to ask me whether I am OK?

'Yes,' she says, her face suddenly softening like a damsel in distress.

'I thought you were a good swimmer...what happened there?' he asks with deep concern in his voice.

'It happens sometimes when you venture into dangerous waters,' I cut in sharply, casting a dagger-glance at Aisha, who is just cowering for cover now.

'Well, you should thank Kairavi,' he says proudly, placing his arms around my wet shoulders.

'I think I'll just go to my room and rest for a while,' she replies without looking him in the eye.

I'm so proud of myself that I can't stop beaming. I've sabotaged her plans and I've shown Aisha her place. Vivian thinks I'm a hero and Aisha must be scratching a pole somewhere.

Ten

*H*ere I am, waiting for lunchtime so that I can see Vivian, when a pretty looking couple walks by. And I am not joking when I say pretty—they look like Barbie and Ken, and they are both dressed in white. They are heading towards a floating gazebo where I spot a priest waiting for them. They are about to get married!

'Aww,' sighs the Thought Bubble wistfully as I watch the most beautiful wedding ceremony of my entire life. They look so much in love, and the way they gaze into each other's eyes as they whisper their vows against the backdrop of the ocean waves and the setting sun is perfect. It is so perfect that it is almost unreal. And at that moment, I have a rather irresistible thought—what if Vivian and I could get married right here. On a white sand beach. Just the two of us?

'And who exactly is going to give him the idea, Kay?' chides the Thought Bubble. Yup, that could be a bit of a bump.

Yeah, marriage is the last thing on Vivian's mind right now, but it would be stupid to let such an opportunity go. I have to talk to him. After all, what have I got to lose? And it's not like we come all the way to the Maldives every day! I just have to be tactful and broach the subject carefully...

It is already close to 6 p.m. and I reckon Vivian must be out of the conference hall by now.

I stride along the coast looking for Vivian. I just have to talk to him about my brilliant idea. They can probably arrange for a priest on order. But it doesn't matter if they can't. Vivian and I aren't too enthu about religious rituals anyway—the important thing is to be together and love each other unconditionally.

I peer into the gym, but I don't see him there. He isn't near the pool either. *Where could he be?* In my urgency, I bump into someone.

'Aisha...what are you doing here?!'

'I could ask you the same question,' she says airily. She is wearing a long pink maxi dress with silver trimmings, looking totally gorgeous. Her streaked hair is tied up in a messy braid which falls lightly over her shoulder.

'Listen, I don't have time for all this. I have to look for

Vivian. It's important.' I turn to walk away.

'Oh Vivian... I don't know where he is. We were just having coffee half an hour ago but...' she trails off innocently.

'Don't believe the lying witch! She is lying...Vivian would never have coffee with her,' screams the Thought Bubble, but its voice is drowned out by the roaring wave of jealousy swelling inside me.

'Oh shut up. He would never have coffee with you. In fact, if he had known you were coming, he wouldn't have come at all!' I say spitefully. *There, that should put her right in her place.*

Aisha lets out a high-pitched laugh that reverberates across the conference hall. 'Oh Kairavi! You are so cute,' she says in between peals of laughter.

'What...what do you mean?'

'I am on the organizing committee along with Vivian. We have been preparing for this for months! Didn't he tell you?' she says with a gleeful smile as she pinches my cheeks lightly.

She's lying. That can't be. Vivian would never...

I can feel my heart sinking. My mind is going numb. Vivian would never...

There has to be a reasonable explanation for this. I scurry up to the room and lock the door behind me, my breath growing shallower and faster every second. *I have to talk to him. Like right now.* As I pace up and down the room, my eyes fall on a bunch of conference handouts lying on the table. I pick up the glossy sheets and flip them around. There, at the back of one of the handouts, are the names and contact details of the members of the organizing committee. My heartbeat quickens to a crazy pace as I pore over the names. There it is—'Dr Aisha Dhawan', right next to 'Dr Vivian de Mello'. I had seen these brochures on Vivian's desk but had never bothered to go through them. I mean why would any sane person go through the brochures of some boring orthopedic conference? My heart lands with a thud at the pit of my stomach and I feel noticeably lighter in the head. So he knew all along. He knew Aisha was going to be here. And he'd been in touch with her all along! Is this why he didn't want me to come?

Was this entire conference just a plot so they could be together here in the Maldives?

'It is very much possible,' rues the Thought Bubble.

OK, just hang on a second here. I can't be dumb enough to fall for Aisha's cheap tactics all over again. She pulled off something similar in Goa and almost ripped Vivian and me apart for good. So maybe Vivian knew she was going to be here. But that doesn't prove anything! I know just how professional he is, and so focused on his goals. Aisha's presence—or absence—probably doesn't even matter to him.

All Aisha needs is a piece of my fuming brains and possibly a whack on her head. And I'm going to give her exactly that. As for Vivian, I'll deal with him as soon as I find him. I'm sure he has a good explanation for all this.

With my newfound resolve, I march in the direction of Aisha's cottage, which is barely a few meters away. *I'll show that bitch who's in charge! She just can't do this to me anymore.* The door is slightly ajar and in my fury, I don't even care to knock. What I see inside shatters me into a million pieces.

No. No. This can't be happening. They can't be kissing! It's possible Vivian went out for a swim and got water in his lungs and Aisha was giving him some mouth-to-mouth resuscitation. *Oh God, please let him have water in his lungs.*

'Aisha! What are you doing?' I bark, and she turns around to look at me, a smug, triumphant look on her face.

Vivian is still in a daze and looks at me with wide eyes, unable to believe that I walked in on them just now.

'Kairavi…please…it's not what it looks like…' he finally stammers, but his words come out as meaningless and hollow. He clearly doesn't have water in his lungs, and that, right now, is rather disappointing.

He's been cheating on me…with Aisha, no less. I am so zapped that I can't even cry. In fact, I have no idea how to react to this. It's not even a figment of my imagination, and it's not something I've assumed. I've seen them going at it with my own two eyes and I've caught them red-handed.

I just can't look at his face right now. I quickly turn and run towards my room, with Vivian close on my heels.

'How dare you? How could you?' I shriek at him as soon as enters the room after me.

'Kairavi, listen…please allow me to explain…'

'Explain?! You have an explanation for what I just saw? You were kissing her!' my voice breaks down. I can't believe this is happening to us. Everything has been so bloody perfect. We had been so much in love. OK, so maybe we didn't get to spend enough time together, but we always had this quiet understanding and trust between us. And I came all the way to the Maldives to be with him…only to find *this*!

'I wasn't kissing her! She came on to me and I didn't know what to do!' he yells.

'Yeah, right!' I say bitterly. If that was really the case, he should have been pushing her off, not sticking his tongue into her mouth. I had no reason to trust him anymore. This was over. Everything was over.

'Kairavi, I love you and only you. You know it. Please believe me,' he says helplessly, trying to collect me into his arms, but I jerk him away. It is too late for apologies and explanations.

I am feeling more angry than heartbroken right now. It's true—all men are the same! I immediately call the reception and ask them to book me on the first flight out while Vivian sits in silence. What else can he do? He has disgusted me to the core and at the moment, I just loathe him. How could he shatter my trust in him so mercilessly?

Suddenly, everything becomes crystal clear to me. This conference was a huge eyewash—he and Aisha had come here to be with each other, while I sat alone at home and pined for him. How clever! Well played!

'I'm going back. Don't try to come near me, or I'll kill you,' I say resolutely as I pack my bags. I reckon he gets my message because he doesn't reply. Instead, he keeps his head hung low and stands silently in the corner of the room. I bet he must be secretly happy that I am leaving. He can now spend all his time with Aisha and lick her ugly gums for all I care. I hope both of them get syphilis and drown in the sea because that's what they friggin' deserve.

It is only when I board the flight back do I realize the magnanimity of the situation. Everything is over. My life is over. *Vivian has cheated on me!*

The jingle-jangle of red bangles seem all the more agonizing, as do the coochie-cooing of newly-weds who seem to be totally oblivious to my tears, along with everyone else around them. All our time together flashes like a slow-mo movie in my head and it just makes me sick in the pit of my stomach. *After all that we had shared…how could he do this to me?! Where did I go wrong? We had everything going for us.* I remember how we met for the first time a little more than a year ago, when I broke my shoulder and got admitted to the hospital. We both just knew that we were meant to be. We were so much in love…Then what went wrong?

Was he blinded by her porcelain skin and endless legs? Is it because I am not as pretty as her?

'Yeah that could be it…' concurs the Thought Bubble. *God, I just hate it!*

But now I know. He cheated on me because he doesn't find me attractive anymore. In fact, he probably finds me downright ugly. That's why he ran all the way to the Maldives. Men are such creeps—every single rotten one of them. Come to think of it, he never really gushed about my prettiness all that much—but at least he had never found me repulsive before!

'Sorry, ma'am, we don't serve alcoholic beverages on this flight,' says the airhostess when I ask for a bottle of wine. *Seriously, what kind of an international flight is this? No alcohol?!*

I want to hate Vivian with all my heart, but I just can't. It is way too painful. I have never loved anyone the way I have loved him. Also, I have never felt so humiliated in my entire life. Oh God, how the hell am I going to survive this?

I contemplate buying myself some duty-free liquor at the airport, but I'm too broke. This trip has cost me much more than all my savings. I really shouldn't have gone at all. What I didn't know wouldn't have hurt me. I would just have been happy to see Vivian back and everything would have been perfect...like before.

'Coulda, shoulda, woulda,' hums the Thought Bubble annoyingly and I just feel like drowning it in a bottle of cheap vodka. *Cheap vodka, yes!*

I ask the sales person to give me the cheapest bottle of vodka available and he brings one from a brand that I have never heard of before. The bottle isn't pretty either. But it is cheap and it has a 50 per cent discount on it, so I take it anyway. You would think duty-free is all about the fancy stuff but nope, this place has something for everyone.

I pour half of the vodka into the bottle of water I got from the flight and fill the other half with water from the cooler outside the washrooms. And then I proceed to collect my luggage, hoping that it has made it to the right destination this time.

By the time I book myself a cab outside, I am already feeling a little light-headed...and better. Vodka can make everything better. I come home to an empty house, which is good, because I'm really not in the mood to speak to Farah right now. She'll definitely ask questions if she sees my swollen face and it will be so humiliating to tell her that

I lost my boyfriend to another woman…who is way hotter than me.

'Oh dear… I don't believe this. Are you sure, Kay?' asks Baani when I tell her everything that happened in the Maldives. I don't believe her; she has always been very fond of Vivian. I wish I wasn't sure. I seriously do. But it all happened in front of my eyes—there's no denying it. Even Vivian didn't have answers…

'Could there be a misunderstanding?' she presses on. She sounds almost as heartbroken as I am.

'No, Baani. I saw it with my own eyes. He was kissing her, right there!' I burst out in loud, inconsolable sobs as soon as I say it. Hearing it aloud only makes it more terrible.

He-was-kissing-her. See how horrible that sounds?

'Hang on… I'll be there in the morning,' Baani says, after she puts me on hold to have a quick word with Kapil.

'Seriously, you will?' I can't believe my ears.

Baani is coming all the way from Goa to be with me. Just the thought of it brings a smile to my face. Fuck Aisha. Fuck Vivian. Baani is going to come and make everything OK…just like old times.

I can barely sleep that night. As the image of Vivian and Aisha locking lips right in my face tears at my insides, I oscillate between periods of helpless sobbing into the pillow and murderous rage. I so badly want someone to talk to—even that creepy Farah will do—but she's never at home at night. God knows how much college kids party these days! It wasn't like this back in our time...

Oh God, I am old and single. This is the end of me. It seriously is.

Eleven

*W*hen I open the door the next morning, I see Kapil standing there.

'Kapil!' I shriek, overwhelmed with mixed feelings. I mean I really like Kapil (now), but I was really hoping to spend some serious girl time with Baani. Kapil is sweet and all that, and he really looks out for me, but he's...well, a little—how do I put it nicely—'uncle-jee types', which is probably why he gets along fabulously with Vivian. I mean these two can talk endlessly about stocks and bonds, the sensex, the new planning commission and basically all the stuff that nobody really gives a shit about.

'I had time over the weekend, so I thought why not. Plus, I had to meet a few people here for work,' he says as he casts a furtive glance at Baani, who is still struggling with her bags near the elevator.

I give him a puzzled look, but then rush over to meet Baani. Just looking at her face makes me feel infinitely better. And she is equally thrilled to see me. God, it has been months since we even had a proper phone conversation! However, I do notice that she looks a bit tired and haggard. Must be the bus journey, I reckon.

Since Baani's old room now belongs to Farah—which Baani is visibly unhappy about—the two of them have to shack up in my room, while I agree to sleep on the couch outside, at least for as long as Kapil is here. I have seen Farah for all of two minutes since I got back, and that too when I had to open the door for her at six in the morning, after which she snuck away into her room and hasn't shown her face since. She's seriously no good. I mean, I have been heartbroken and miserable these past couple of days and she hasn't even noticed!

Later, when Baani is in the shower, I catch hold of Kapil and ask him what that funny look was all about.

'Eh…nothing. She's just been acting a little weird these days so I couldn't trust her to travel alone,' he says with a worried expression on his face. *Baani acting weird?* Now, that's news to me. And I know Kapil. He's known Baani for decades and he wouldn't just make that up on his own. He loves Baani to bits and he would do anything for her.

I really want to hug Baani and ask her what's wrong but at the same time, I want to let her bring it up herself.

'Seriously, there has to be something wrong with your thermostat. You are like a water balloon you know,' says an exasperated Kapil after Baani asks him to switch off the air conditioner because she is too cold. Incidentally it was she who asked him to lower the temperature, because apparently she was 'drenched in sweat' just five minutes ago. I can see the tears well up in Baani's eyes and her chin is quivering.

'You called me a water balloon...you think I'm flabby... and wobbly...and...'

'No no no... I meant it strictly in terms of temperature sensitivity...' says Kapil in panic as he rushes to collect a very angry Baani in his arms. This must be serious because I know Kapil does not like PDA at all—another thing he has in common with Vivian, not that it matters anymore. In fact, he uses the word 'sambhog' (which is Sanskrit for 'copulation') because he is just too shy to say that he's got the hornies. Baani finds it very annoying while I find it amusing—but that's only because I am not at the receiving end of the aforementioned 'sambhog'.

'But you meant something else,' she wails and Kapil throws up his hands in the air.

Oh Baani...poor thing. What's got into her? She's always had it so together, and now she's just falling apart. I really need to catch hold of her and have a good hard talk. This is not like her at all... I mean water balloon? Come on!

The next morning, I walk into Baani's room after Kapil has left for work, only to find her sitting on the bed with an ashen face.

'Baani, what on earth is wrong? You have to tell me.'

She just looks up at me blankly.

'Shit! Don't tell me you are still upset over the water balloon thingie!'

'I'm pregnant, Kay!' she says, her voice quivering.

I stand stunned for a moment trying to register that piece of news.

'Well, isn't that awesome! Baani, I'm going to be an aunt...isn't that awesome!' I squeal.

This is indeed great. Fancy Baani becoming a mom. Oh, I'll spoil the kid silly. I'll be the cool, spoiling, doting aunt and all that.

'Kay, I'm not ready... I don't think I can handle being a parent right now.'

'Oh shut up, Baani! You'll make a fabulous mom. I've always known it. You are smart, sensible and patient—you'll be great. Oh God, I'm so excited! Umm…have you told Kapil yet? What did he say? Is he thrilled? I know he must be thrilled.'

I'm blabbering away because I just can't contain myself.

'No. You've seen how things are between me and Kapil… we always seem to be fighting these days.'

'But that's different! There's nothing wrong with your relationship. It's only you who has to…'

Oopsies…wrong timing!

'I have to what?' asks Baani indignantly.

'N…nothing…you have to be patient and make it work. It will work, don't worry,' I stammer.

'That's not what you were going to say, were you?'

Oh drat! This woman knows me too well.

'OK…well…' I start. Maybe this is the right moment to address the elephant in the room. But I cannot use the word 'elephant' lest she starts bawling again.

'Baani, of late I've noticed that you're being too hard on Kapil,' I say with a straight face.

'I'm hard on Kapil?! Whatever makes you say that?' Her eyes are wide with astonishment, but I can tell that she's trying to absorb every word I'm saying.

'You guys had such a special bond…what happened?' I ask, giving her a chance to present her side of the story. *God, I should be a shrink. I'd be so good at it…asking open-ended questions and all that.*

'It's all his fault. He's not taking this marriage thing seriously at all. He still behaves like we are boyfriend and girlfriend, you know.'

'And what's wrong with that?' I ask politely, although I'm tempted to bombard her with all those 'how not to let your marriage come in the way of love' kind of headlines in *Cosmo*.

Come to think if it, it's a very first-world kind of problem.

'I'm scared, Kay...it's a baby. Like a whole person to take care of!'

'It's all right! It'll be a joy,' I say, but in my heart, I know her fears are not unfounded. My thoughts go back to Ronan and the roller-coaster of a ride he gave me the three days he was here. And by roller-coaster, I only mean it in the nauseating sense of the thing, not the fun part. And that was just for three days.

Kids can be downright horrible at times, like this neighbour's kid who has a steady stream of snot flowing down his nose all the time. And God, the way he screams!

Yes, babies are scary...isn't that why they use them in horror movies so often, and their toys too? But I bet Baani's baby will be different...it's going to be cool and awesome like her, except if it gets Kapil's genes. Then it will become a matter of acquired tastes, entirely.

They might look cute in pictures but in reality, they are

not the most pleasant creatures to be around. But that's not what Baani needs to hear right now. She needs support and encouragement. And things did work out between Ronan and me in the end, didn't they? Hell, he even said he didn't hate me. That would mean that he totally loves me. Isn't that an achievement? And he does kinda smell nice when you hug him...

'Everybody has babies and everybody survives them,' I say, failing to conjure up a more positive image. 'And some people even go to the extent of having another one, so it can't be all that bad, no?' I say encouragingly.

Baani nods her head even as she has a faraway look in her eyes.

Just then, I hear the door click and peer out to find Farah entering the house. Her hair is disheveled, she is clearly hungover and her mascara is all over the place.

'Baan, come outside. I'll introduce you to Farah,' I chide on, unsure of whether it is a good idea at all. But I just want to take Baani's mind off the stress she seems to be crumbling under.

'Why is that thing wearing leather pants at eight in the morning?' Baani whispers into my ear.

'This is the usual time she comes back home after partying all night,' I whisper back and Baani pouts and nods slowly, with one of her eyebrows raised inquisitively.

We suddenly feel like two sad, middle-aged aunties who

thoroughly disapprove of young people having fun even though we've done all that and worse, back in our days.

Baani and I walk into the kitchen, where Farah has filled up the blender with gourd and is now about to perform the despicable act of pulping it and downing the goo at one go. I can already feel nausea swelling up inside me—it happens every time she does that in my presence. I've even rescheduled my breakfast just to escape this misery.

'Farah, this is Baani. She lived here before…'

'Oh, so it was you…' says Farah haughtily, eyeing Baani from head to toe. This chick is seriously weird. I now kinda feel apologetic for making Baani meet her. Meanwhile, Baani is looking at me with a what-the-fuck-is-this look on her face.

'Come here, Baan, I have to show you something,' I pull Baani by the arm and usher her out of the kitchen.

'Really? Really, Kay? Are you seriously living with this crazy person?' asks Baani as soon as we enter my room and close the door behind us.

I shrug in response, and then we both burst out laughing.

I haven't seen Baani laugh like this since she came here. We spend the afternoon bitching about Farah, because I know bitching is the antidote to everything—even unplanned-pregnancy-induced panic attacks.

Twelve

I'm so glad I have Baani and Kapil around to take me through this, even if Baani is a hormonal wreck right now. But I don't blame her—I've read about pregnant women going berserk and I have seen them in movies too, and I know it will pass. She just needs some TLC, and some alone time with Kapil so that both of them can prepare to enter this new phase of life together. In a way, it's good that they came here. They are finally getting to be by themselves, which Baani tells me is rarely possible at home with the overenthusiastic in-laws hovering around all the time.

Revealing the news of impending fatherhood to Kapil was rather uneventful. He was overjoyed, but there was no drama. He didn't question Baani, and he wasn't upset that

Baani kept this humungous thing from him all these weeks. That's another thing he and Vivian have in common—they are boringly non-reactive people, and very matter-of-fact about everything. No extreme emotions at all.

However, this pregnancy thing must have been a lot to take in, considering that it was a contraceptive failure, but I know Baani will make a great mom. And I will be the most awesome aunt in the whole world! In fact, this whole episode is definitely helping me take my mind off Vivian and from what he did to me.

Oh and I know what I'll do. In the evening, I'll somehow talk Kapil into taking Baani out for a movie or something. I know how much she misses good 'ol Mumbai and some time out with Kapil will definitely do her some good.

'But we can spend time here too,' Kapil insists.

'Kapil, oh Kapil. Have you even an ounce of romance left in you? Your wife is pregnant; she needs some pampering and support. Is that so hard to do?' I yell at him and his face shrinks. Something about his expression tells me that he is getting my point. You see, with Kapil, you always have to spell these things out. He is totally incapable of coming up with such fairly obvious ideas on his own.

Baani, like always, does not want to leave me alone

because she, after all, came here 'to be with me'. I assure her that I'll be fine and literally push her out the door. They are barely gone an hour when the doorbell rings.

Oh God, please let it not be another fight! I sigh and open the door, fully prepared to send them out on their way again, but my heart misses a beat when I find Vivian standing there.

'Why have you come here?' I ask coldly with my arms wrapped around myself.

'Kay, please hear me out. I didn't...'

'Don't give me any of your shit, Viv. You cheated on me!'

'No, Kay! I would never do that. And you know it!'

Frankly, this conversation isn't going anywhere. And I don't see any point taking it any further.

'Kay, let's get married,' he says impulsively just as I am about to slam the door on his face.

'What the hell are you saying?!'

'Let's get married. You know I can't live without you.'

'It's a trap! Don't listen to him,' whispers the Thought Bubble, but my mind is too boggled to make any sense of the situation. Here we are, at the brink of a full-on breakup and *now* he wants to get married? Talk about timing!

I stare at him bemused, waiting for him to explain this sudden epiphany.

'Kay, let's get married...let's be together. Isn't that what you always wanted?'

Oh, is he going to play the appeasement card with me now?

Dangle a carrot and watch me hop over to him with saliva dribbling out of my mouth. No, sir! I'm not going to fall for any of this bullpoop anymore.

'Do you really believe I am that desperate to get married to you?' I shoot back.

'You are not, I am,' he replies. 'Please come back...'

He looks tired and defeated, but I have no sympathy for him right now. Every time I look at his face, I am reminded of that scene in the Maldives and it instantly fills me up with rage and loathing, for myself and for him. As for Aisha, she has always been loathsome, so no extra loathe points for her. And I suddenly realize I have been stupid to blame her, when Vivian has been making himself out be the low hanging fruit. *He* is the one who broke my trust, not Aisha.

I really have nothing to say to him right now.

I bang the door on Vivian's face and storm inside the house.

'You should have at least talked to him!' Baani is livid when I tell her that Vivian was here and that I slammed the door in his face. It was a painful thing to do when what my heart wanted was to pretend it was a nightmare and rush into his arms. But there is such a thing as self-respect, and I happen to have it. He just cannot get away with what he's done. In fact, he should be grateful that I love him enough to not plot nasty revenge on him, or else he would have been dead, or at least severely crippled, by now.

'There is nothing left to talk about...' I retort, but Baani just shakes her head disapprovingly.

'You know, maybe it was not his fault after all,' Kapil butts in.

I am not sure whether these two are my friends or his. *Why are they siding with him?!*

'Why is it so hard for the two of you to believe that he cheated on me?' I ask bitterly.

'Because...because...' says Kapil, exchanging a furtive glance with Baani and I instantly know they have been up to something. I cock an eyebrow at them, waiting for them to spit it out.

'Because...we went to meet him and he said Aisha came on to him and he was caught off guard...and then you came in. And it was all a case of bad timing,' Baani blurts out.

Now it's my turn to be angry. They said they were here to support me and they went into the enemy camp? *This is sedition!*

'How could you?!' I demand, only to be met by two very guilty pair of eyes.

'Listen, Kay...give him a chance, please. He deserves it,' Kapil reiterates.

'Why?'

'Because he loves you!' Baani chimes in. 'Are you really going to trust Aisha over him? Don't you want to give him the benefit of the doubt, especially when you know what Aisha is capable of...'

My breathing slows down for a bit. What if Baani is right? What if I have been wrong in my judgment? What if this is another one of Aisha's stinky conspiracies?

I look at Baani and Kapil, who are looking back at me expectantly with unwavering conviction in their eyes. My heart wants to believe Vivian, but I just can't get myself to forget that scene. *Am I letting anger cloud my judgment?*

'I need some time alone,' I tell Baani and Kapil, and walk out the door. I really need to clear up my head, and think rationally. Maybe I'll take a long walk and think this over with a calm mind.

I spend a good hour walking briskly across Bandstand, and spend another hour sitting and staring at the grey Arabian Sea and the Mumbai skyline. People are whizzing past me, oblivious to my presence. *What do you really want, Kairavi Krishna?*

I wish I wasn't so confused. I love Vivian and will always love him, but what about the humiliation he subjected me to? He's made me feel loved like never before, but why did he not tell me that Aisha was going to be in the Maldives? If he wanted to be with Aisha so bad, why didn't he just dump me and go to her? Why did he come all the way to Mumbai to be with me when Aisha always had the hots for him...and he knew it? If he loves Aisha, why does he want to marry me now? Or is it his way of washing off the guilt?

Oh God, I wish I had some answers. I wish I had some sort of a sign. I swivel around to head home when I bump into a strong, masculine chest, and a waft of citrus cologne fills my nostrils. Vivian. I know it even before I look up to see his face. His eyes are boring into mine and I quickly look away.

'Are you going to walk away from me?' he asks in a low throaty voice that just makes my knees wobble.

'I'm... I'm not sure,' I stammer.

His gaze is steady and unflinching, and I finally muster the courage to match it.

In his deep brown eyes, I see all the moments we have shared and all the love we've had for each other. I don't want to let go of all that. Those eyes don't lie. I know it deep in my heart. We stare into each other's souls in silence even in the midst of maddening crowds and incessant traffic noises, and awkward as it may look to a passerby, I find it strangely comforting. My tense muscles loosen up and my body involuntarily draws closer into him. His arms curl around me in a tight embrace, and for the first time, he isn't giving a fuck about his no-PDA rule. He buries his face in the crook of my neck and we stand entwined in each other's arms as the sun sets against the ocean and the city begins to light up. I don't know for how long we stay that way, but it feels warm and fuzzy and soothing, like a homecoming, and everything feels alright again.

Thirteen

*B*aani can't hold back her squeals when she sees Vivian and me walk into the house together, and Kapil is so overwhelmed with emotion that he just leaps at Vivian to hug him. Sometimes I feel these two would do well as a couple—they have so much in common!

'We're moving in together!' I shriek, my face flushed with excitement.

The room is suddenly very noisy with everyone shouting, laughing and screaming with happiness. Well, not everyone, just Baani and me. Vivian can't keep his hands to himself and he's behaving like he hasn't seen me for decades. *Oh God, I feel so light and free.* Everything is finally alright again, and it feels like a heavy weight has been lifted off my chest.

Ravi has been wanting to meet Baani so I have invited him over too. It is going to be a big, grand party—just like good old times in Goa. Baani too seems to be in a much better mood now. She is cheerful and relaxed, and apparently some of it seems to have rubbed off on Kapil as well. Ravi, as usual, is his crazy self, yapping all over the place and poking Baani in the tummy. But he stops immediately when we tell him there's a little person inside.

I glance over at Vivian and we exchange an amorous smile as everybody else is busy filling up their glasses.

Next week I'm going to move into his apartment, and I am so excited! We are finally going to be living together—like a *real* couple! And we're going to talk with our respective families—basically just Mom, Dad and Jacinta—to plan the wedding.

It's going to be a court wedding, we've decided, followed by a dinner at some fancy restaurant with family and close friends. At first I thought it was a boring idea, but then, even if I do have a typical Big Fat Indian Wedding, who am I going to invite? I realize that at this point, I don't care about the 'wedding' per se. The important thing is we are getting married and that's what I have always wanted.

Where there is joy, there naturally has to be a joy-buster, too. Farah suddenly decides to make an appearance right in the middle of the revelry and all eyes turn at the same time to look at her.

Oh God, someone please drill some sartorial sense into this girl.

She is wearing a plunging top that is supposed to accentuate her cleavage, but all that is visible is her ribs. And just about everything that can be wrong is wrong with her hot pants. Camel toe? Seriously?

Baani and I exchange knowing looks, but we don't let out our sniggers. *Oh no, we are better than that.* At the same time, we can't steal our eyes away from the original Chanel bag she is carrying.

'Wow, that bag must have cost a bomb,' says the Thought Bubble, and I am suddenly filled with a strange kind of envy, considering that my closet is packed with cheap rip-offs from Colaba Causeway. Not that they aren't pretty…

'Now who's this?' Vivian whispers anxiously into my ear.

I haven't told him yet that I had rented out Baani's room. Otherwise he would ask *why*, and that would make me sound really crazy. And he would just get mad at me for letting some random person in, even if it is just a harmless wiry college kid with a pathetic sense of fashion.

'Umm…she's a friend's friend…just shacking here for a few days,' I say hastily and Baani shoots me a puzzled look. I send across a telepathic signal to her, pleading her to play along, and thankfully, she gets it. I feel terrible for lying to Vivian, but we've just gotten together after our huge fight and I don't want him to think that I pawned off half my house just so that I could chase him to the Maldives, because that would sound insane.

'Hellloooowww there, have we met before?' Ravi asks in a creepy sing-song voice as he swaggers over to Farah.

I can see the Thought Bubble sigh and roll its eyes dismally. Somebody should really ban that pickup line forever.

Farah looks visibly bothered by his overtures. 'Uh hi,' she says awkwardly and shuffles over to the entrance of her room.

'No seriously, I feel like I know you from somewhere... from another lifetime?' Ravi carries on unperturbed.

I think I should intervene. I don't want my flatmate to think that I hang around with creepy people. Ravi may be a nice guy, but he has never been particularly known to keep his emotions in his pants.

'Farah, you must be tired...' I signal to her and she quickly slinks into the room and shuts the door behind her.

Ravi turns to look at me as if I have betrayed his trust or something.

'You'll hit on anything that moves, won't you?' I hiss into his ear and pinch his arm till he yelps.

'But I think we've met before!' he whines.

'Ya, ya, of course,' I say sarcastically. 'From another lifetime? Seriously, Ravi?! Try something original next time. Perhaps something less creepy...'

'No, I meant it literally. I *have* seen her somewhere, but

I can't seem to place her...!'

I look at Ravi bemused. Now where could he have met her? He lives at the other end of the city and hasn't been this side since we last met. And Farah hasn't been in Mumbai for more than a month.

'That's not possible, Ravi. Maybe you are confusing her with someone else,' I tell him off and he shrinks back into his seat grumpily.

The topic is soon forgotten as everyone gets back to the drinking and chatting and eating. I snuggle up close to Vivian and wrap my arm around his. He responds by planting a quick, clandestine peck on my forehead. Sometimes I just love it when he is so awkward with these things in front of people, although it can be quite irritating at other times, like when we are watching a movie.

Even with all that noise around me, I am perfectly at peace with myself. I'll never let him go, I think to myself.

Ravi hasn't mentioned Farah since, but I can't help but notice that he is unusually quiet throughout the evening. He's probably figuring out ways to hook up with her. Typical Ravi.

Just then Farah emerges from the room. She has changed into a wine-coloured Juicy Couture tracksuit now and is looking a lot less skanky. She conveniently ignores the five of us in the living room and heads to the kitchen, probably to conjure up another one of her lethal, ungodly concoctions.

She practically lives on this shit—I've never ever seen her eat real food since she began living here.

I notice Ravi peering over curiously.

'If you are attracted to her, you should go see what she's having for dinner,' I whisper slyly and Baani bursts out in giggles. I realize I'm not half as mean when I am by myself, but Baani's company somehow brings that out in me.

'I'm not attracted to her,' Ravi retorts defensively. 'I mean yeah, she's hot and all that, but I'm just trying to recollect where...'

'Oh please, get over it,' I cut him short. Ravi has just been going on and on like an old vinyl record.

Kapil and Vivian have taken to discussing some very uninteresting stuff about polls and possible alliances between parties and it is clear that those are the only kind of parties they genuinely care about. I mean today is such a big day—and this is what they want to talk about?

I've learnt to ignore this because I've got so used to it by now. Plus, Vivian and Kapil are meeting after a long time. Got to give these two soul sisters that much leeway.

Just then my phone beeps. It's a message. 'Wanna spend the night at my place? Today, tomorrow and forever?'

I look up at Vivian, trying hard to control my grin, which is threatening to spread like wildfire across my face. He looks at me with a slight smirk that no one else apart from me can make out.

'How can he be so romantic in the middle of discussing politics with Kapil?' wonders the Thought Bubble.

'What about Baani and Kapil? They came here for me.' I text back, although spending the night away from him is the last thing I want to do today. I have missed him like hell! And I haven't yet had enough of his touch, his caress and his familiar comforting scent.

He draws a sad smiley and makes a face at me before diving into his phone to type out another message.

'In that case, I'm not going back tonight!'

'Wheeee...' yells the Thought Bubble and my cheeks turn warm in a very pleasant kind of way. It's perfect—we'll shack up right here in the living room, and Baani and Kapil can have the room to themselves. I can't wait to be alone with him, snuggle into his body and talk in whispers all night. It's been so long!

Maybe this whole temporary breakup thing worked out for the best. Everything feels so fresh and new again, like it was the first time we met. You know what they say about post-breakup sex, don't you?

Fourteen

After Ravi has left and Baani and Kapil have retreated to their room, Vivian and I finally have some precious moments together. There is so much to say and so much to share that it is almost overwhelming. I don't even know where to start. Vivian slowly draws his face closer to mine until our lips brush against each other. My heart flutters, as if it were our very first time. He nibbles my lower lip ever so gently and slides his arms across my waist pulling me into him. As his tongue probes my mouth further, I find myself overcome with a strange kind of emotion—one that I have never experienced before. I instantly pull myself away from him.

'Why the fuck did you do that?' demands the Thought Bubble angrily.

But the truth is I am as clueless about this as the next person.

'What happened, Kay?' asks Vivian, looking quite alarmed at my reaction.

'Did you kiss Aisha the same away?' I don't know what makes me say that. A demon spirit, perhaps? The words just fly out of my mouth, with no censorship whatsoever. The weird thing is that I seem to have no control over them.

'I thought we were over this,' says Vivian.

I can clearly see the hurt and disappointment on his face. *Oh God, what have I done! I shouldn't have. I really shouldn't have. I'll apologize...and I'll never do it again.* But...but all I can see right now is the haunting image of Aisha bent over his face with her lips locked with his. It just doesn't go away!

'You still doubt me, don't you?' he asks in a low voice and I just sit blankly in response. I know I should just say, 'No, I don't. I'm sorry... I didn't mean it,' but I can't bring myself to say those simple words, which would fix the situation right now. I don't even reply in the affirmative, because frankly, I am not sure how I feel. Do I trust him completely? If I do, there should be no 'ifs' and 'buts'. If not...then well, I don't! I so badly want to trust him, but I can't stop myself from wondering how he felt being close to Aisha. Did he enjoy kissing her more than he enjoys kissing me? Did he feel a 'connection' of some sort? Does he find her more attractive? Of course, he must...have you seen those legs?

Oh God! This is going to drive me crazy. I have so much going on inside me, but I can't seem to be able to articulate it in words.

'Good night,' he says finally, and flips over to the other side to sleep, leaving me to stare blankly at the ceiling.

When I open my eyes in the morning, he is already gone. *Shit!* I groan and fall back into bed. I really didn't mean to say whatever I did last night but I Just. Couldn't. Help. Myself! I know it was a terribly pathetic thing to do, but...

How am I ever going to get over this Aisha episode?

I know what—I'll apologize to him as soon as he comes home today.

'Are you sure he's going to come home?' asks the Thought Bubble and I am suddenly overwhelmed with self-doubt. What if he doesn't turn up and goes back straight to his place?

I decide not to tell Baani about what happened between Vivian and me last night, or she'll just worry herself silly. Baani and Kapil have to leave for Goa today and I don't want to do anything that will stress them out—especially Baani, because she's finally happy and smiling after such a long time. And she's pregnant...

I plaster on my best fake smile and walk towards the

bedroom to see whether Baani and Kapil are up yet. I can hear noises from their room, so I proceed to knock on the door. However, before I can lift my hand, the door swings open and Baani emerges, her face fuming in anger.

'What happened?' I ask hesitantly, but she just rushes into the kitchen to douse her temper with a glass of water. I turn my gaze towards a hapless-looking Kapil, who just shrugs even before I can ask him any questions.

'I didn't do anything!' he protests in a whisper.

'I can hear you!' Baani yells from across the hallway and I find myself caught in a strange early morning crossfire.

'He doesn't even want to be around me anymore!' she yells on, her gaze directed at me this time.

Kapil just stands quietly in a corner. I look towards him for an explanation, but I guess he's too flummoxed at this point to provide me with an answer. I grab him by the arm and pull him into the room. These two need a rap on the knuckles.

'I just asked her if she wants to stay back here with you for a few more days, and she exploded in my face!' he finally blurts.

'She's been so happy and relaxed since she came here, so I thought spending some time with you would do her good,' he goes on with a sullen face.

Poor Kapil. He always means well, but has the soft skills of a wooden table. I can almost imagine him putting his point across in a cut-and-dry manner, and Baani being a ticking hormonal time bomb these days, coming up with an entirely innovative interpretation.

I throw my hands up in frustration, but then decide to take a few deep breaths and summon my inner saint before I head out to tackle Baani.

'Babe,' I begin as I wrap my arm around her. She still looks worked up and I can still feel the tension in her muscles. 'He just said that because he thought you were more at ease here. He is really concerned about you, Baan!' I say softly. She hrmphs and looks the other way, but I can tell that my words have not been lost on her. She sits grumpily on the couch, while I wait for her to say something. Is this what marriage does to couples? I wonder meanwhile.

'I don't know, Kay! I just tend to overreact sometimes!' she finally bawls, hiding her face in her palms. I've never seen hormones wreak havoc like this before. But at least she's self-aware, and that's a good thing.

'So do you want to stay back for a few more days?' I ask her gently. 'If you think it helps your stress levels?'

'No yaa. I think I'll head back. I can't keep running away from things like this. And you guys just got back together—there must be a lot of catching up to do,' she says with a wink.

Right now I don't have the heart to tell her what

transpired between Vivian and me last night. She's already such a bundle of nerves and quite on edge.

But I'm happy that both of them have now come to terms with the impending parenthood, and seem quite kicked about it, albeit a little anxious.

Fifteen

Although Baani and Kapil have taken up all my emotional energy, I can't stop feeling fidgety about last night. I think of calling Vivian, but then decide against it. I know how busy he must be in the OPD and he usually doesn't entertain calls at work, even if they are mine.

Sorry about last night. I didn't mean it.

There. An SMS is so much easier and less awkward. At least I don't have to wait for his immediate response. He can go over it again and again, and then decide that it wasn't such a big deal after all. Shit like this happens all the time between couples, and I am jealous of Aisha only because I love him and can't bear to see him in the arms of another woman. I let out a sigh of satisfaction, as if a huge burden has been lifted off my chest. The ball is in his court now...

The house suddenly feels empty and lifeless without Baani and Kapil. Once again, I have no one to talk to, but I have a couple of new projects that need my urgent attention. I drag myself to my desk and am just about to start working on them when my phone rings.

Vivian. My heart leaps with excitement. It isn't usual for him to call during work hours, but maybe he saw my message.

I look at the screen expectantly and my face falls. It is Ravi. *Drat!*

'Listen, about that chick in your house, something is definitely shady about her,' he says in a serious voice, skipping all pleasantries.

'Get over her, Ravi,' I snap rolling my eyes. When it comes to women, this guy can be annoyingly persistent.

'I'm not joking, Kay. I can't recollect where I've seen her, but I have a bad feeling about her. You need to investigate.'

Investigate?

'What do you mean investigate?' I ask incredulously. I can sense the tension in my own voice, although I am not sure if there is any reason to be alarmed. Ravi isn't the most sure-footed person I know, but at the same time, he wouldn't fool around with such things.

'I mean check her stuff...raid her room...whatever.'

'What?! Are you mad?'

I'm not going to raid her room. That would be ridiculous!!

'OK, suit yourself, babes,' he says casually and disconnects the call.

If it wasn't for the ongoing hairfall problem, I would rip out a clump of my hair in frustration. Everything...just everything is going wrong in my life. Why is everyone hell-bent on annoying me?!

I think I'll just go downstairs and buy myself a super-sized ice cream cone because, what else is left to do? Moreover, food makes everything hurt less. Especially sugary food.

I'm just browsing the supermarket on my way back and who do I run into? Ratna aunty!

'Kairavi! Where the hell have you been?' she squeals as she hugs me tight. Just so you know, Ratna aunty is a close friend of Mom and is the poster woman for spinsterhood. She lives in a tiny one-bedroom apartment with twenty-three cats, of which Sherni was one.

I always thought of her as the sorry single woman who roamed around with uncombed hair in a house full of cats, but today she is looking livelier than usual, what with the red streaks in her hair and a generous coat of makeup.

'Aunty...you look...different,' I manage to blurt out. I really want to give her a more enthusiastic, heartfelt compliment, not because she is extraordinarily sweet, but because she totally deserves it. But for some reason, I just can't digest her in this new ensemble. Although it is quite fab, I must say!

'Well, thanks!' she says airily. 'It's good to see you too! I was actually meaning to call you after that day.'

'Which day?' I ask curiously.

'Your flatmate didn't tell you? I came by couple of weeks ago to ask after you. I even left a note with that girl.'

That's weird. Why didn't Farah tell me? I hope she didn't tell Ratna aunty that I was in the Maldives, or the news would reach Mom and I would be dead meat in no time.

'Err...maybe she forgot! I'll drop by at your place sometime soon, Ratna aunty...and I'll get Sherni too. I'm sure she would like to meet her old friends,' I say cheerfully, knowing fully well that the only way to bond with this woman is to talk incessantly about felines and related stuff.

'Yeah she did look a bit lost to me, and her boyfriend was around too, so...'

Farah has a boyfriend? I never knew of one! And she gets him home when I am not around! That's rather sneaky. I'm not sure I am entirely comfortable with the idea.

'Really? I didn't know she has a boyfriend!' I ask nonchalantly, hoping Aunty would spill more details without me having to sound too nosey, and worse, clueless about my own flatmate.

On cue, Ratna aunty leans in towards me as if to let me in on a deep dark secret. 'She does!' she whispers ominously, 'and he seemed quite old...kinda in his 50s, I think.'

A boyfriend in his 50s!

'Are you sure it was not her dad?' I ask, flummoxed.

'Well...didn't seem like, going by the chemistry and all that. You know what I mean...'

'Wow. That's an interesting piece of news,' I mumble meekly, quite shocked at the revelation.

A boyfriend twice her age! This Farah girl must be nuts! Anyway, it is none of my business who she goes around with. I'll just warn her not to bring strange men inside the house when I am not around.

I have coffee with Ratna aunty and give her the complete update on Sherni, which she listens to enraptured, and then I head home to have a good, long talk with Farah.

When the door clicks shut way past midnight, I know it is Farah. Although I am half asleep, I know there will be no better time than this to catch hold of her. I stumble out of bed and walk into the living room rubbing my eyes, when something blindingly bright and dazzling stuns my vision. It is an enormous diamond necklace dangling from her neck! What the...

'Wow...that thing is huge!' is my first and immediate reaction.

'Thanks!' chirps Farah, although I have no idea why. I clearly didn't mean 'huge' in a nice sort of way. That thing around her neck is downright ugly!

'Where did you get it?' I ask, hoping against hope that the girl didn't spend all her pocket money on this vulgar-looking monstrosity.

Her hitherto cheerful gaze now turns shifty. 'It's a gift,' she says briefly.

Of course, a gift from the elderly gentleman! How could I not have guessed? He's the one who's been giving her all these designer goodies. Her confession confirms what Ratna aunty said. So *this* is why young girls date men who have one leg dangling in the grave!

I quickly snap out of my thoughts. 'Yeah, about that, Farah, I would really appreciate if you don't bring your boyfriend here when I am not around...or even if I am,' I say curtly.

'I don't have a boyfriend,' she replies with the straight face.

'Oh come on, you don't have to be embarrassed. I'm not going to judge you or anything (*I totally will*)! It's just that I like my privacy,' I say in a softer voice.

'I am single and no one comes here,' she insists. *Oh God, why doesn't this girl just come out and accept it. He's just old, not dead!*

She looks at me as if I have lost a nut or something.

'I came to know that someone was visiting you here a couple of weeks ago. And you didn't even tell me that Ratna aunty left a note!' I go on.

'That...that was my father,' she says in a low voice after a moment of thought, but her shifty eyes completely betray her. I know she is lying through her teeth. *Why is she not telling me the truth? Why does everyone keep lying to me?!*

Could it be possible that it really was her dad that day? But what about the 'chemistry' that Ratna aunty was talking about? She surely must have seen something. Unless...

Eww. Eww. Just Eww. Just the thought of it makes me sick to the stomach.

'Cool then. Just know that I'll be watching,' I say finally, pushing the rather disturbing father-daughter-doing-hanky-panky-on-the-couch imagery out of my head.

The warning has been duly served and if I catch her doing anything sneaky, I'll just ask her to leave. I've had it with her anyway. She's supposed to be my flatmate, but she's not really adding much value to my existence.

Anyway, I don't have time to bother about Farah's fossil of a boyfriend. I have to start packing my stuff because I'm going to be moving in with Vivian! I've been staying over at his place every now and then, but 'moving in' has a nice official kind of ring to it. It is almost like living as a married couple.

Whoopsie daisy! If I am going to move out, what am I going to do with Farah? I don't really want to throw the poor girl out, but she can't keep living here forever. What if Mom-Dad come visiting? I haven't even told them that I let out Baani's old room. And that too, illegally!

I know. I'll give her a proper notice period and all that. She certainly can't stay here all by herself. And it is best if I talk to her right now so that she has enough time to make arrangements.

I walk over the door of her room and gingerly knock on it. No reply. I knock again. Still no reply.

'Farah?' I call out, but she still doesn't respond. I am suddenly filled with a sense of foreboding. I know she is inside, then why isn't she responding?

Is everything all right?

With a slight bit of trepidation, I turn the doorknob and the door swings open. There is no one inside. Drat! She's out again…and she just got in a few minutes ago! Some social life this girl has. I allow myself to feel a little envious. I hardly have any friends left in the city and I barely have anywhere to go to, except for some odd dates with Vivian. In fact, I was enormously relieved when Ravi got back from Singapore—imagine, things were *that bad with my social life*!

I have never been inside Farah's room till now, because she always locks it before leaving, but mostly because I didn't really care. Guess she forgot to do that today. I look around and am instantly taken aback by the mess—there are clothes everywhere, and food crumbs on the floor and the desk. There could very well be a dead body rotting somewhere under the clutter and no one would come to know, because of the overwhelming stench of decaying food. I scrunch my nose in disgust as I spot a half-finished box of pizza under the bed. But there are a few things that look like they don't quite belong here—Prada, Gucci, Louboutin, Jimmy Choo, exotic perfumes that you don't get in India...you name it and this girl has it. There is a Cartier watch sitting on the dressing table, along with piles and piles of MAC makeup and cosmetics from expensive brands.

I remember seeing the occasional designer handbag on her. But this? This is like Disneyland for women, even if it smells like a public urinal.

'Something is really off here,' whispers the Thought Bubble and I have absolutely no reason to disagree at this moment. When I met her first, she never looked anywhere close to loaded. Unless she won a lottery or something.

Seriously, what is the deal with this girl?

...That chick in your house. Something shady about her... Ravi's words ring ominously in my ears. Was I wrong in dismissing him so casually? What if there really is something horribly wrong with her? And I never even cared to check! What if I am *gulp* harbouring a criminal in my house? I could get killed! Shit!

Should I call the police? Or Vivian?

'And tell them what?' interrupts the Thought Bubble and I quickly backtrack from that idea. I have to sort out this mess on my own, that much is certain. Should I check her stuff? No, that would be really unethical, I tell myself.

'Better guilty than dead,' urges the Thought Bubble and I begin to see the point. If I have to find out the truth about her, this is my only chance.

I bolt the main door from inside so that she'll have to ring the doorbell when she gets back. I then tie a scarf around my nose, sprinkle some essential oils on it for survival and dive right in. Let me tell you that navigating through all that clutter is no mean feat, but I spend one whole hour in that pigsty looking for clues. I fumble through her wardrobe and gasp momentarily at the price tags still hanging from some of the dresses.

Stay focused, Kairavi, I remind myself every now and then and carry on with my mission with newfound determination. This mystery needs to be cracked.

And then my eyes fall on something that makes me skip a breath...

Sixteen

The next day is Sunday, so Vivian helps me move my stuff over. I decide not to carry much, since his is a one-bedroom bachelor pad, and we anyhow plan to look for a bigger house to live in after the wedding.

'I hope this is enough for you,' he says as he flings open the sliding door of a large wardrobe. I notice that he has crammed all his stuff into a couple of small drawers at the bottom and left most of the place vacant for me. Seriously, it is these little things about him that melts my heart every time I am with him. We haven't talked about the unpleasant moment again, mostly because he never brought it up. I reckon my apology was accepted and the case stood resolved. I promised myself that I wouldn't let anything like that happen again. We were finally back together and everything was perfect like before—I couldn't afford to screw it up all over again.

I hug him in gratitude and proceed to arrange my stuff on the shelves.

'Is that girl going to live there forever?' he asks casually. I know he is referring to Farah and I can't help but cringe a little.

'What happened?' he asks again.

'Time to fess up!' says the Thought Bubble and I am filled with a strange mix of nausea and dread. OK, where do we begin...

'Umm...actually...there's something about Farah that I want to tell you...' I start off.

Vivian is listening to me intently with his head cocked to one side and his long fingers rubbing his stubbled chin.

Oh God, he looks so gorgeous. We should be having sex right now instead of this stupid discussion about Farah. I smack myself mentally and gather my thoughts, which seem to be bouncing all over the place.

'What? Is she troubling you?' Vivian offers helpfully, noticing my silence.

'I think she might be an escort,' I say flatly. Seriously, there is no better way to say it. No point beating about the bush either...

'What?! Are you crazy? How can...you said she is a friend's

friend...' he yells, looking visibly confused and miffed.

'Well, I may have lied about that...' I confess in a low guilty voice.

'So are you saying that you don't know her?' His voice is still loud and I can see the frown lines forming on his forehead.

I shake my head, averting my gaze and looking at the rug under my feet. Vivian runs an exasperated hand through his hair and lets out a long sigh while struggling to take all of this in.

'And how do you know she is an escort, Miss Sherlock?'

I slip a hand into my pocket and fish out a visiting card which has Farah's close-up on one side and 'Pleasure Escort Services' written on the other. The name on the card says 'Babydoll', but it has Farah's mobile number printed underneath.

Vivian lowers himself on the sofa and buries his face into both his hands.

'Why did you have to take her in? What was the need?' he asks softly, trying hard to maintain his composure and not yell.

Uh oh, that's a toughie. I decide I'm not going to lie anymore, even if it makes me come across as a freak.

'I wanted the money to surprise you on your birthday,' I say.

Vivian is stunned into silence. His mouth is agape and

he just looks at me with exaggerated disbelief in his eyes.

'This is by far the stupidest thing you have done, Kay,' he says after a couple of minutes. Boy that hurts!

'What did you expect for this? A medal of love?' smirks the Thought Bubble. Indeed, why was I even expecting him to be impressed, when I had landed myself into such deep shit?

'But escorts are also people. They too deserve a home?' I say in my defense, not fully sure as to what I am really getting at.

'Are you serious, Kairavi?!' Vivian's voice is now much shriller and I can see that whatever I am trying to do is doing nothing to quell his anger. 'Do you even realize how dangerous this could be? First off, it is illegal...and how do you know she is not getting clients into the house? At best, you could go to jail for this, and at worse, get killed!'

I stare at him, at a loss for words, and I can feel tears pricking my eyes. Why does he have to yell so? After all, I did it for him...does he not understand?

'Why? Why was it so important to come to the Maldives? We could have celebrated my birthday after I got back!'

'But I...'

'Kairavi...you risked your safety. And for what?'

At this point, I am beginning to lose my cool. 'For what?' He may be right about that. I may have risked my safety to make his birthday special, but what did I get instead? His face stuffed in Aisha's mouth! *And that is why he is yelling at me now.*

'You are right. I shouldn't have come and spoiled it for you,' I say angrily.

'Spoiled what?' He looks back at me, confused.

'DON'T!' shrieks the Thought Bubble.

'Your honeymoon with Aisha...that's what! That's the reason you are so angry about all this, isn't it?' I hiss.

Vivian stares at me for several moments, shocked out of his wits. Finally, he turns around and walks out the door, slamming it behind him...rather loudly. Which is so unlike Vivian. I mean, Vivian never does this kind of a thing, regardless of how bad his mood might be. He's usually this oasis of calmness and composure in the middle of a crazy, chaotic world.

I must've really pushed the wrong buttons—perhaps all of them at once. I realize I am getting better at this. Getting better at driving Vivian away from me. But I have no clue why I'm doing it or if I can do something to stop it. This insane jealousy and rage every time that incredibly painful memory flashes before my mind's eye—I just can't seem to do anything to block them out. Or at least shut the fuck up about it, even when it overpowers my mind.

And the most disconcerting thing about all this is that I'm not feeling all that guilty about what I did. Sure, I feel bad about rubbing it in his face, not once, but several times, but he sort of asked for it, no? He should've thought twice before letting Aisha make her way into his oral cavity like a black cloud of demonic smoke, if at all that's what it was.

I curl up on the couch, a bundle of anger, hurt and guilt. A part of me knows I'll have to apologize for my irrational behaviour, but that's definitely not going to happen right now.

That night, both of us go to bed in silence. This has never happened before.

'This is a bad sign,' rues the Thought Bubble, and I can feel something clench within my chest. Vivian and I had agreed we'd never sleep over a fight and true to our promise, we never did. In fact, we hardly even fought. *God, what have we done to ourselves! This is all Aisha's fault, that scheming, conniving... BIATCH!*

I turn around to face Vivian, hoping he'd be awake, but he's facing the other way. We've never, ever slept facing away from each other. Even when we weren't making love, our faces would always be close, breathing the same air, our limbs entwined. I miss his warmth and I wonder if he misses it too. I tiptoe out of bed and walk over to his side, peering over to see if he really is asleep. He seems to be. He usually sleeps soundly after a long day at the hospital. I quietly bend over to plant a soft kiss on his forehead. Just as I am about to walk back to my side of the bed, his hand reaches out for mine and tugs it gently. I turn around to face him, but he is in deep sleep. He hasn't spoken to me since my outburst and I am dead sure he wouldn't have held my hand if he wasn't REM-ing. Nevertheless, I stand still for a while, taking in his warmth before he wakes up and pulls away.

'You have to trust him,' the Thought Bubble pitches in out of the blue. Like I need unsolicited advice at the moment. It's not like I don't trust him. I do, but…'BUT?!'

Seventeen

*I*t has been two whole days and we haven't talked. This is major, and has never happened before. We are supposed to be the couple that never sleeps over a fight, I remind myself, but the pact has been broken. All this is new to me, and saying that it's making me uncomfortable and anxious would be a gross understatement right now.

Maybe I should just apologize to Vivian and set it right. Let's face it, I can't be away from him for too long, and his sullen face tells me he is just as troubled. And angry. More angry than troubled right now though. I admit I had no good reason raking all that up when it had been done and dusted with.

'Oh, Baani... I feel dead. So dead inside,' I lament over

the phone as soon as Vivian leaves the house.

'Shut the fuck up, Kay. Enough with the drama already. The only parts dead about you are your hair, nails and possibly some skin on your soles. The rest of you is OK, really. Stop wallowing in self-pity!' Baani shoots back.

Sometimes I really wish Baani would indulge my blues for just a little longer. I mean she does give me a shoulder to cry on for a good while, but then she always gives me a tight whack on the head at the end of every sob fest. I admit I need that at times, otherwise I could go on being the Misery Queen forever.

I realize I need to introspect. A lot. My emotions have been getting the better of me lately, and even though my head knows, that my suspicions are baseless, the incident has deeply scarred my heart. I've never had such a hard time getting over anything in my entire 26 years of existence. I replay every little moment spent with Vivian and every little heartwarming thing he's ever done for me, and I realize that our relationship is way too precious to lose. I can't afford to kill what we have just because of my unfounded insecurities.

That evening, after a day of hard self-talk, I decide to have a heart-to-heart with Vivian, with a firm resolve to leave all of this behind for good.

I pace about the house all day waiting for him, and as soon as he enters the house, I cling to him like a little puppy.

He doesn't say anything, but he runs his fingers through

my hair. 'That's a good sign,' infers the Thought Bubble. His touch warms up my insides and I begin to feel more at ease. Things are not so bad after all.

'Can we talk now?' I whisper, still holding onto him.

He nods gently. I hover around him as he freshens up and changes into something comfortable. He's obviously tired, but when else will we have the talk if not now? We need to put this behind us as quickly as possible. After all, we are living together now and are about to get married.

'So I thought about it a lot…' I start reluctantly as we both settle to sit on the bed.

He cocks his head to one side, listening to me intently.

'I know I messed up, Viv. I was really irrational about the whole thing. I know it wasn't your fault at all…and that you weren't cheating on me, but I just had a hard time getting it out of my system. I hope we can forget all this and move forward without any baggage.'

'You're the one carrying the baggage, Kay. Not me,' he says. 'I just hope you'd trust me a little more. The way I look at it, what we have isn't so weak, or is it?'

At this point, I have only a heartfelt apology to offer. I have clearly hurt him, and I really need to get a grip on my volatile emotions. That's what adulting is all about, isn't it? And if Vivian can do it so well, why can't I?

I draw myself closer to him and he opens up his arms to take me in. And just like that, everything goes back to normal again. We spend the evening talking, laughing and cuddling as if nothing has happened. Little do I know that my ghosts aren't about to leave me anytime soon...

Eighteen

The next morning, Vivian is scuttling about the room getting ready for work while I am still lazing around on bed. It just feels so natural to be like this, as if there never was a time when we didn't live together under the same roof. I could really get used to waking up next to him every morning.

'Decided what to wear for tonight's party?' He smiles at me through the mirror as he brushes his gorgeous brown hair.

'Party? What party?'

'Oh, did I not tell you, Kay? There's this gala at our hotel to celebrate the success of the conference, and I would love it if you came with me.'

OK, so he has clearly forgotten to ask me out on this supposed 'date' and it is too short a notice to mentally prepare myself for a party packed with bone doctors, but whatever. I am happy that Viv wants me to be a part of every facet of his life, and it is time we start attending public dos together—after all, that's just how relationships progress from one stage to another, don't they?

Vivian plants a warm little kiss on my forehead before heading out the door, and I somehow manage to haul myself out of bed. After all, fishing out an appropriate outfit for a formal evening is no small ask. I rummage through my limited inventory and finally settle on a red knee-length bodycon dress—sophisticated and sexy, all at once.

I really can't wait to go to the party with Viv. As insignificant as it may sound, it is a milestone in our relationship. This is the first time I will be formally meeting his doctor-crowd.

'You need to sound smart,' reminds the Thought Bubble. But I'm the least bit nervous. I know a thing or two about fractures and I'm sure I'll be able to make reasonable small talk there.

Blame my excitement, but I am all showered, dressed up and ready to move an hour before Vivian comes to fetch me. Of course I don't tell him that, because it would, you know, just look desperate? I wear my best nonchalant face over all that makeup and gracefully slink into the co-driver seat right next to him.

'Somebody's looking sexy as hell!' he exclaims after giving me a longish top-down look. That's one of the many things I adore about Viv—he never lets any of my dressing-up efforts go to waste. Not that I've dressed up for him as such, but a little validation never hurt anyone.

The party is at The Oberoi—one of the poshest hotels in Mumbai—and by the time we drive into the curb by the entrance, I start to feel little flutters of nervousness in my tummy. Without me having to say a word, Viv walks right up to me, twirls his arm around mine, pulls me close enough that I can feel his warmth and smell his familiar scent, and walks me past the doors. Everything seems a million times easier with him by my side, and at some level, I also feel a little smug walking into a fancy do with unarguably the hottest orthopedic in Mumbai on my arm.

While I make a beaming entry through the door, it doesn't take long for the devil to steal my smile, because who do I spot right across the room? Aisha fuckin Dhawan! She slithers through the poshly dressed sea of doctors in her silverish gown, and nonchalantly throws her arms around Vivian to plant a peck on his cheek, completely ignoring my presence. I can literally feel my innards go up in flames, but I decide to play it cool.

'Hi, Aisha! What a surprise to see you here!' I flash my fakest friendly smile at her.

'Oh well, I should be the one feeling surprised. After all, you are the one who is the, what's the word for it, non-doctor here. Ha ha, just kidding,' she places one of her clammy hands on my shoulder and a wave of nausea takes over me. I realize that her fake smile is faker than mine, but there is no way I am about to exit this game.

'I thought it would be nice for Kay to meet everybody here. After all, these are the people I work with,' Vivian intervenes in a feeble attempt to diffuse the situation.

Even though Vivian sticks by my side throughout the party, introducing me to people, I feel a little lost and distracted throughout. It doesn't help that Aisha is trailing along with us wherever we go, like an unwanted third wheel, and to make things worse, Vivian is being his usual nice and polite self, which is only encouraging her more.

'It would be quite uncool to throw a fit, you know,' whispers the Thought Bubble, and I am forced to agree. Vivian and I have just survived a longish relationship crisis and have emerged stronger. The last thing I want to do is screw it all up by coming across as a jealous, over-possessive bitch.

We somehow survive Aisha's onslaught, but on the way back home, I sense that Vivian is a little distracted. 'All OK?' I ask him casually, and he doesn't even hear me the first time.

'Huh?' he mumbles. 'Ah yes...yes... I guess I am just a little tired, that's all. It's been a long day.' It's pretty apparent from his demanour that his mind is somewhere else, and although it feels a little weird, I let it pass.

We reach home, change and freshen up—and all this while Vivian seems to be present, yet not. He slips into bed alongside me and instead of nuzzling into my neck like he usually does, just rolls over and falls asleep.

'Something is definitely off,' warns the Thought Bubble. I throw myself on my pillow and stare at the ceiling fan as Vivian snores softly right next to me. What could it be, I wonder to myself.

My thoughts are interrupted by a gentle vibration and I realize it's Vivian's phone lying in between us. My radars go up in smoke when I see Aisha's name flashing on it! I have half a mind to answer the call and give her a piece of my mind for calling my guy so late in the night, but I'm not sure of what to say. The call goes unanswered and then, a message flashes on the screen. I can't read it because the phone is locked, but by now, my mind is flooded with a million possibilities. *What on earth is going on here? I thought we were way past this.*

In a weak impulsive moment, I do the worst possible thing I could have possibly done. I lift Vivian's finger as gently as possible and use it to unlock the device. My fingers tremble as I swipe my way to his message inbox, but I keep telling myself that this needs to be done to settle things for once and for all.

'I really miss our times together, Viv. And I know you do too.

I could see it in your eyes tonight. See me soon?'

I sit there trying to process what exactly these words mean. Are they still together? Does Vivian still have feelings for Aisha? What does she mean by 'saw it in your eyes'? He was with me for the entire duration of the party. Did they manage to steal glances even then? Do they meet often behind my back?

I am grappling with these questions and more when a hand comes forward to take the phone from mine. It is Vivian. He is wide awake and staring at me in disbelief.

'What do you think you are doing, Kay?' he asks me in a hurt voice.

I look down at the phone, trying to point him towards the message that I just read. He reads it coolly.

'Are you cheating on me?' I mutter, for lack of better words.

He doesn't reply.

'Listen, Kay,' he says after moments of silence that seem like eternity. 'We have gone over this many times, and quite honestly, I am tired of justifying myself every single time. If you find it so hard to trust me that you have to do what you just did, it is better if we part ways.'

His words hit me like a thunderbolt, and it is only in that moment that I realize that I, not he, has been the one to break the bond of trust between us. But it is too late. The damage has already been done.

Nineteen

It's been close to a week since I last spoke to Vivian and moved back to my apartment, and one random morning, I realize I can't get my butt out of bed. My body feels heavy, and my head heavier. For no particular reason, I feel like bawling my lungs out. OK, there might be reasons, but they certainly do not warrant this level of melodrama.

Truth be told, I haven't felt this pathetic ever. I instinctively reach out for my phone to dial Baani because she's obviously my first go-to person in times of crisis, but then I stop myself. Baani has been battling quite a lot of stuff of her own and she's finally beginning to sound like herself. I can't possibly trouble her with a rant, and that too so early in the morning.

'Mom!' I bellow over the phone and almost break down. At least it's just Mom at the other end, which means I can be as pathetic as I want to be, without having to pretend to have it all together. Because frankly, right now I am nowhere near 'held together'. My insides are in shambles and I just can't seem to get my thoughts in order.

'Listen to me, Kay,' Mom's voice is gentle but firm. She is not particularly known to indulge my misery. 'You need to get out of the house and get yourself a life. Moping around the house all day is doing this to you,' she says a little sternly.

There we are—it's something I've kinda, sorta, most certainly known, but you sometimes need a rap on the knuckles to get yourself moving. Although I miss having a prolonged discussion with Baani over this, where we'd dissect every emotion down to the last fragment and then spend some quality time overthinking everything and then feeling a little more miserable, before we finally decide to snap out of it and decide to bury the demons the old-fashioned girly way—over a tub of ice cream and a soppy movie. Or, if the crisis is really huge, we might even get our hair colours changed.

But Mom's technique is not too bad either—quick and painless, albeit a little abrupt. I somehow haul myself out of bed and into the shower. I frankly have nowhere to go and no friends I'd want to visit, either. Maybe I'll sit alone in a coffee shop and write some poetry.

'That's just lame. Since when did you start writing poetry?' butts in the Thought Bubble.

Well, since right now. I'm sad and that's what sad people are supposed to do. Write poetry. It's supposed to be therapeutic and all that, or so I remember reading in *Cosmo*. Or maybe not. That will just make me feel worse. If not writing it, then reading it definitely will.

Oh I know what I gotta do—I'll spend the day at Blue Cross. Yes! There couldn't be a more perfect thing to do. And I haven't been there in ages. I quickly pull on a comfortable pair of jeans and an old T-shirt, because you know, things can get pretty messy when you're handling sick, injured and abandoned animals. But despite the smell of poo and animal hair all over you, there's a quiet joy, an inexplicable peace that comes with seeing the unadulterated love and trust in their eyes for you. That's the kind of thing you'll never get to feel with another human being.

Twenty

My life seems to be falling into some semblance of order, or so it seems. It helps to hang around at Blue Cross, and Karan sometimes meets me there and we catch a coffee or something afterwards. It is fun being around him. And easy.

'I think I might need a favour from you,' he starts one day as we sip on our respective cold coffees at a bistro near my house.

I cock my head to one side out of curiosity. I am in a pathetic state myself. Of what possible help could I be to another person?

'So there's this little project I volunteered for, and I need someone to help me with a photoshoot. As in, be the model. It's for a beach-cleaning campaign I'm doing with an NGO.'

Eh. Me, a model? Whatever made him think I'd be the right person for the job?

'Are you sure you want me in the pictures? I mean, don't you know any good-looking people?' I jibe, and he shoots me an annoyed look.

I knew that he has no taste for my self-deprecating humour, but there are times when I just can't resist it.

'Well, if it means anything to you, I would like someone real in those pictures.'

'Real is just a euphemism for ugly, isn't it?' I laugh. He clearly isn't amused.

'So are you going to help me out or not?' he asks impatiently.

'OK, I'll do it,' I say, rolling my eyes. It is no biggie, really, and for all the kindness Karan has showered on me over the past few weeks when I was down in the dumps, this is the least I could do for him.

'Look into his eyes. They look infected with love,' sniggers the Thought Bubble and I have never felt more annoyed at it. Here I am, doing this fabulous photo shoot and generally having a great time with a friend, and this bloody guy has to butt in and spoil it all with that icky L-word.

Dammit, I sound like a cynic. Or maybe the cynics had

it right all this while. Love is just a euphemism for 'things are about to get majorly fucked up, and will take your brain along with them.'

Nevertheless, I do take a moment to peer into Karan's eyes. He is half focusing on me, and half on the background, probably trying to get the right angles for the photo shoot.

'Hey, Karan…' I call out to him, quite purposelessly. His gaze shifts to me and I see his face transform right before my eyes. *Dammit!* It instantly goes softer, the frowns ease up, a silly smile spreads across the breadth of it and those eyes—oh man, those eyes! They really do look infected…with love!

Shyte! This can't be good. We are such good friends. We have the most awesome time in each other's company. This is just going to screw up everything.

'Well, maybe not. Karan is a great guy and…' whispers the Thought Bubble sneakily, much like the hypnotic Kaa in *The Jungle Book*.

Shut up. Shut up. Just shut up!

What I absolutely don't need right now is a rebound affair. I've been in enough of those to know that they are a sure-shot recipe for disaster.

'Kay, is everything OK? You look…err…worked up?'

Gawd, why does everything have to show up on my face like that! Why can't I be like one of those people who could be plotting a murder in their head and at the same time, have the facial expression of a child relishing an ice cream? Well, come to think of it, there wouldn't be much difference between the two if you were planning to murder the right person.

Aisha's dastardly face flashes inside my head and I quickly realize that this is the worst time to be thinking about her. I need to look all happy and cheery and upbeat for the photo shoot—after all, we are doing this for a good cause.

'Yes, yes, all OK, Karan,' I reply, pulling myself away from the murderous thoughts involving Aisha. And also ice cream. Had it not been for her, Vivian and I would still be together. That creepy conniving witch…

Focus on looking cute, Kairavi! I remind myself and instantly straighten up my face. Karan probably thinks I'm a freak. In fact, I am quite sure of it, because he told me that so in so many words the other day, when he caught me talking to myself in the mirror. That it was the rear-view mirror of his car only made the situation worse.

We finally wrap up the shoot and drive over to my place. It has been a long and tiring day, but oddly satisfying. It has been a while since I have done something meaningful with my life, because all my energy over the past few months was wasted on Vivian and associated problems.

'Thanks for helping me out with this, Kairavi,' Karan says.

'Well, to be honest, I should be the one thanking you. I think I needed this more than you did. It feels refreshing. It really does,' I tell him. 'I had been through days of moping around in the house, and I wasn't really motivated to step out until something like this gave me a good hard push. Truth be told, it did help take my mind off things, even if for a little while.'

'Is it OK if I come upstairs to drop you?'

'I'm not a baby, Karan!' I laugh, but he insists.

We park the car near my gate, and he quickly dashes out of his car seat to hold the door open for me. I find that a bit odd, because who on earth does that in 2020? I feel a little obliged to return the courtesy by asking him to stay back for a cup of coffee.

'Ooh... What was the delicious thing that just left?' Farah croons as soon as I plonk back into the sofa after closing the door.

Delicious thing? I am not quite sure how I feel about my friends being objectified so, but hey, this is Farah, so anything goes.

'His name is Karan. We volunteer together at Blue Cross,' I reply curtly.

'Hmm. I'm happy you are meeting new people. It will help you get over... Oh sorry, I shouldn't have brought that up.'

I look up at Farah and she looks genuinely repentant for

digging out the old skeletons. Well, they aren't even that old yet. Just a few weeks old at most. In fact, they are not even skeletons—just rotting corpses of broken dreams and love, backstabbed by betrayal.

'Kay! Stop it!' yells the Thought Bubble and I instantly snap out of the morbid thoughts. Some days my mind really is a graveyard of shitty feelings. Not that I dig it this way. Yuck! I really must stop lamenting over the bygones and bury these stupid graveyard jokes.

Oh and by the way, I decided to let Farah stay back, because all in all she isn't a bad kid at all, just a little weird. And her choices don't really reflect on who she is as a person. She is nice to hang out with, and even helpful at times, even though she doesn't have to work too hard at getting on my nerves. But the main motive behind my decision was something else—I wanted to prove a point to Vivian.

'And what point is that?' queries the Thought Bubble innocently, but I know that at this moment, I just want to be a bitch to him.

Who the hell does Vivian think he is, trying to tell me what to do and how to live my life when he himself thinks nothing of cheating on me...and that too in the Maldives?!

'Really? That's your entire point?' The Thought Bubble is right. I don't have a point, at least not yet. But I have an annoying roommate. Yes, that's what I have.

Sometimes I really feel like taking some kind of sedative

to at least block out some part of my brain. The Thought Bubble part, for example.

'Well if you want, we can go out somewhere?' Farah offers sweetly and I imagine myself tottering behind her in my couch-potato clothes and messed-up hair in some shady pub. Or maybe I'm just stereotyping her. *I shouldn't. I shouldn't.* But that doesn't change the fact that she is dumb and annoying and not the kind of company I'd like to keep at the moment, although she's trying to be really helpful and all that. God, I miss Baani so much right now!

'Thanks, buddy, but I'd rather stay home,' I reply politely. 'Oh, tell you what. I think I'll Netflix and chill,' I announce. That's what all the cool kids these days are doing, apparently.

I notice a weird grin spread across Farah's face.

'What now?'

'Netflix and chill?' she says, still grinning stupidly and making me doubt myself for a moment.

'It's about watching movies right? On the laptop?' I confirm.

'Yeah that's Netflix. But who are you going to chill with?' she teases and I'm borderline pissed off and very much inclined to fling a vase at her. What is she trying to do here—rub salt into my wounds?

'Alone, obviously,' I say proudly. 'All I have to do is get myself a subscription and prop myself on the sofa with some snacks.'

'You've been propped up on this sofa for days,' butts in the Thought Bubble and I want to smack it on the knuckles, even though it might be true. But hey, I'm going through heartbreak here. I am allowed to be a sad vegetable and wallow in self-pity. *Cut me some slack, will you!* I hiss inwardly.

Farah laughs out loud and vanishes into her room, closing the door behind her.

I sense something fishy and quickly Google 'Netflix and chill' and end up feeling mildly embarrassed and heartbroken. And old. I am so senile now that I don't even know Internet slang anymore. Maybe I should stop talking to all these young people, because I'm just going to make a fool of myself. Moreover, it has suddenly hit me that I have no 'chill' in my life, and that makes me feel sadder. This isn't helping at all. My youth is whizzing past and here I am, drifting alone and aimless.

I need ice cream. I know it is old-fashioned, but at least it works and one can go at it alone. I call up the neighbourhood grocery store and order a big tub of Oreo cookie-flavoured ice cream.

Just the sight of it makes my world feel brighter and happier. The little specks of chocolate in the white-creamy goodness.

'Emotional eating alert!' beeps the Thought Bubble, but I ignore its warning. This is not the time to be thinking about calories and other such useless stuff. My heart is broken, for fuck's sake. I need ice cream.

I play *P.S. I Love You* for the umpteenth time. I know the movie like the back of my hand, so that even if my mind drifts off in between, I would know when to cry even without paying much attention to the dialogues.

'If your pity party is over, can we get back to getting a life?' demands the Thought Bubble as soon as I open my eyes. I didn't realize I'd conked off in the middle of the movie. The ice cream tub lies on my bedside, all melted. I pick it up and glug it down as a gesture of rebellion, and quickly realize how pathetic I am being at this moment.

'You know what, maybe you should give this Karan guy a chance. He's nice, and he really seems into you,' suggests the Thought Bubble, in a very faint voice—not the usual sarcastic, overwhelming tone I am accustomed to. I am forced to give it a thought. There is nothing wrong with Karan, really. He's sweet and kind and we have so much in common. And he's cute too. If I go at it with an open mind, this might actually lead to something nice. Let's face it, Vivian and I are done for good. And clearly he seems to have moved on. Then why should I be the one brooding and clogging my arteries with tubs of Oreo ice cream? I need to get myself a life. And a boyfriend.

'Also a job,' pitches in the Thought Bubble.

Yes, yes. A job too. I snap back.

I pick up the phone to call Baani.

'You. Are. Not. Getting. Into. A. Rebound. Relationship. Right. Now!' I can already hear her yelling from the far end of the phone even before I've dialed her number. I decide against it. Maybe I'll tell her when something concrete materializes between Karan and me. If at all it does.

One of the things I really like about Karan is his unconventional choices. He isn't really your standard, run-of-the-mill guy. Which is probably why we are here at Catmosphere on our very first 'proper date'. I am not even sure if I can call it that, because it certainly doesn't feel like that—you know the flutters, the excitement and the works? But at least he has chosen a great venue—it is this newly opened cat café right here in Bandra, and it has 25 resident kitties. The menu is a little bleh, but nobody really comes here for the food.

'I love this place!' my face lights up as a grey Persian walks right up to me as soon as we enter.

'Well, to be honest, a lot of thought went behind it. I thought there could be no better way to celebrate our common love for animals,' he smiles back. 'Also, there are cats here.'

Both of us burst out laughing. Conversations with Karan are never a struggle. He is intelligent and creatively inclined, which makes it a lot easier for me to share things with him.

He is kind and he understands my need to move slowly into this.

Although it is supposed to be a date, it feels like any other outing we'd routinely have, just that both of us are better dressed this time around. We chat about our careers, our passions and our dreams for the future. We already know each other reasonably well, so thankfully, we do not have to go through the typical questions that are standard protocol for every 'first date'. Heaven knows I am so tired of that. Probably for the first time, I notice that he has a very warm vibe about him, which draws both humans and animals to him. Even the grumpiest cats in the café get pally with him in no time, which, in my opinion, is far greater validation than what you could get from any human.

'See, that wasn't so bad, was it?' asks the Thought Bubble, and I must admit, the day has been fun. Karan is great company and there is no end to the things we can talk about. I just needed to open up my heart and let him in, that's all.

'We should hang out more often,' I say with a casual smile.

'I totally agree. I love being with you, Kay,' he replies and pulls me into a hug.

I find myself reluctantly hugging him back. I'm just

about getting used to the warmth of his body when he plants a peck on my forehead. There is something different about his expression now. It's softer, and he has that look in his eyes. Is he going to kiss me? 'Looks like,' says the Thought Bubble.

Well maybe I should kiss him back, I tell myself, even though my heart and soul are screaming in protest. We stand near the stairway right next to my apartment, our eyes locked. His glazed with love, and mine, perhaps, with confusion.

He's a nice guy. And I do like him, I tell myself. 'But you don't have to force yourself to love him,' comes a voice from somewhere deep inside me. And this time, it's not the Thought Bubble. *Too late.* I already feel his lips on mine, and they feel like just that—a pair of lips. His arms are wrapped around me, but his touch doesn't penetrate my being the way Vivian's did. I sense a surge of conflicting emotions rise within me, and pull away awkwardly.

'Sorry, I don't think I'm ready for this,' I whisper, almost apologetic for possibly hurting his feelings.

'I understand, Kay,' he says with a smile belying his eyes, and gives me a brief hug before making his way to the elevator. 'Thank you, Kay. Thank you so much!' he says and bends over to plant his lips over mine.

Wait a minute. What the...

He gives me a quick peck and pulls away just as quickly.

OK, so it was a platonic one. Phew! Not the kind that involves the exchange of oral fluids.

'Oh well...that was not needed,' I mumble awkwardly.

'I'm sorry. It just...'

I can see that his face is on fire already. He's probably more embarrassed than I am, which means we should pretend it never happened. What happens in the apartment lobby stays in the apartment lobby. I bid him adieu, and what I see next makes my eyeballs pop out of my sockets and roll onto the floor.

Twenty-one

'Fuckety fuck!' shrieks the Thought Bubble rather dramatically. There, standing right outside the elevator, is Vivian. I'm not sure how long he's been there, but something about the look on his face tells me that he's seen us kissing. It was a pathetic excuse of a kiss, but whatever. I think of walking over to him, but before I can gather my senses, he's already turned around and disappeared into the elevator.

I groan and hide my face in my palms. The Universe is definitely conspiring against me. I'm so sure of it.

'Something wrong, Kay? I said I'm sorry,' Karan offers helpfully and I can't decide whether to be mad at him. I mean what was he thinking, trying to be over-affectionate and all that?! And why did Vivian have to walk out of the elevator right then?! *What would Vivian think!*

'Umm...you guys are no longer a couple. How does it matter what he thinks?' intercepts the Thought Bubble. Yeah, for once, it is right. Why should it matter anymore? He didn't care when he went all the way to the Maldives to make out with Aisha, so why should I?

I literally want to scream my lungs out till my voice echoes across all floors and all the neighbours come out to tell me what a brainless jerk I am. God, I am never going to live this down!

'Karan, I'll see you later,' I say politely instead, trying hard not to let the chaos in my head make itself apparent.

'You sure we're good?' he asks, concerned.

'Yes, sweetie. We're as good as can be.' I give him a tight hug before packing him off into the elevator. A whiff of citrus hits me as the elevator door opens. Vivian's cologne. *Damn!*

I walk into my room and throw myself on the bed, face down. Why on earth do all these freakishly nasty things have to happen to only me? As if it isn't bad enough that we broke up, now he had to see me fake-kissing a guy. This is an emergency. Baani has to be called. I'm going to stay all cool and calm, I promise myself. I take a deep breath—or rather several of them—and dial her number.

'Hey!' I say extra cheerfully. 'How's the bump doing? Started knocking over furniture yet?'

'Go easy on the lame humour,' reminds the Thought Bubble. Cool, stay cooool, I remind myself.

'What is wrong, Kay?' Baani demands in a matronly voice.

'Wrong? Nothing's wrong! Why should anything be wrong? I just called…generally.'

'You can fool the world, girl, but you can't fool me.' *Damn.* This girl already has the mommy hormones flowing inside her. Even her voice sounds…err…mom-like. 'Come on now. Out with it,' she demands.

I start off really well, narrating things very clearly in a calm, composed voice, feeling secretly proud of myself. I am adulting in real time, keeping my emotions in check and all that.

'So? You saw him kissing Aisha and he saw you kissing Karan? Sounds pretty fair to me,' Baani concludes.

'But I wasn't kissing Karan! I just told you, Baan!' I yell and without warning, break down. 'There goes nothing,' sighs the Thought Bubble.

'Now, that's my Kay. I was wondering why you weren't being all Drama Queen about it,' Baani says coolly.

Huh, only if she knew my noble intentions behind putting up the fancy façade. And anyway, what the hell has gotten into her? She sounds like she's achieved Zen or something. The last time we'd met, she was worse off than a wet cat in terms of edginess.

'But why did he have to be there at that exact moment!' I bawl on.

'Well, one plausible explanation could be that he came to meet you, since there are only two apartments on that floor and the other one is vacant?'

I called her up to feel better and she is only making me feel worse. And guilty. But there's one thing I have to admit—her coolness game is A-level and I sincerely hope she isn't faking it.

'Hmm,' I mumble, feeling a little stupid now and embarrassed. It isn't an entirely unfamiliar feeling, considering how many times I've been a doofus in the past coupla months.

'How's your health, Baan?' I ask, feeling a little calmer.

'It's a lot better. I've been practising yoga and stuff. It's not entirely overrated you know.'

Oh so that's her secret—yoga. Now, who would have thunk.

'Just two more months to go!' I manage to squeal excitedly. And she squeals back. Talking to Baani does manage to distract me for a while. In two months, she will be a mom, and I will be the cool aunt doting over the little one. I really hope it's a girl. Don't get me wrong—I'm not gender biased that way, but the other day, I saw this adorable collection of princess-y dresses and sparkly shoes for baby girls. The baby boy clothes were pretty sad in comparison. It will be no fun shopping for a baby boy. Baby girls also get to have pretty clips, hairbands and frilly socks.

Farah hasn't come home in two days and I am genuinely worried. She hasn't told me where she's going, and even her phone is switched off. As annoying as she may be, I must admit that I have begun to feel a little responsible towards her.

'She must be with one of her clients,' suggests the Thought Bubble, and that thought makes me even more uncomfortable. *Is she safe? Where could she be? Should I call the police?*

I decide to wait till evening, and spend the day impatiently pacing about the house, trying to distract myself with some TV shows, but my thoughts are constantly drifting to Farah. At last, around eight in the evening, the doorbell rings. I rush to open it and there she is—looking all happy, with an unusual radiance about her. Before I can ask her whether it is love or Dove, she flings herself at me and smothers me with a tight hug.

'What's the big occasion?' I ask coolly, trying not to make my worry lines show.

'I have to tell you something important,' she says excitedly and pulls me by the arm to the couch in our living room.

Oh God, please don't tell me she's getting married. I'll be the only one left to die a lonely spinster!

'I quit my business,' she says, her eyes as wide as her smile.

'Business? Err…what business?' I fumble. I can't let her know that I know. But from the way she looks at me, I can tell that she knows that I know that she knows. *Oh hell!*

'Don't act up, Kay. You know what was going on. And yet you let me stay here. I'll always be grateful for that.'

I ho-hum awkwardly and roll my eyes inwardly, hoping she'll do my share of the speaking, too.

'Well, my family was under debt so I had to take this thing up on the side. Of course, my parents would have killed me if they found out, but that's the least I could have done for them. I've managed to pay off the loan and now, I don't have to do it anymore.' Her voice is ringing with delight and there is a sparkle in her eyes I have never seen before. I feel happy and sorry for her at the same time. Sorry because she had to make that choice given her circumstances, and happy because she no longer has to do what she doesn't really want to. I momentarily think of asking her if I can keep one of her Prada bags. But maybe now is not the right time.

I pause for a few minutes, trying to figure out an

appropriate reaction.

'Well, this calls for a party! Let me take you out for drinks tonight!' I am genuinely glad and relieved to see her back home safe and sound, and even happier that she has decided to leave her past behind. An evening out in town would do me some good too, I reckon.

'Awesome, Kay! I'll just get dressed!' she squeals like a college kid, which she actually is. It is only now that she is behaving like one.

'You look great,' I comment.

She is already decked up in a flowy red dress and high-heeled pumps, her hair straightened out and makeup in place. How much more dressed could one get? I, on the other hand, have been moping around the house in grey PJs and a tattered grey tee, looking like a cloud of doom. If I am to stand anywhere within a few feet of this girl, I'll need a serious overhaul. A shower will be a good place to begin, I decide. In between scrubbing the blackheads off my face and conditioning my hair, I strategize my makeup. I saw this cool video of some nude-cherry eye makeup, which is supposedly quite a rage right now. Maybe I'll try that out—it will sit perfectly with the beige bandage dress I am planning to wear. If nothing else, at least my eyes will stand out. I even have false eyelashes lying around somewhere. *Hell, I am about to bring sexy back!*

I quickly hop out of the shower and blow-dry my hair, which, as usual, defiantly stands up on end because of the static. But I manage to tame it down with some serum. *Time to get started on the eye makeup.* I watch the YouTube tutorial one more time just to make sure I get the procedure right, and follow it to the T with much enthusiasm, being all careful with the quantity of the product, et cetera. Unfortunately, by the end of it, I look like someone with a rare inflammatory eye disease. How the hell do these women manage to do it! 'Don't worry, it will all fall into place once you stick on those falsies,' says the Thought Bubble helpfully, and I proceed to do the same. Indeed, my eyes look much better now. Quite diva-ish, actually! But those things are bloody heavy, or maybe eyelids aren't really meant for any weightlifting. Oh well, as long as it looks hot, there's no reason I should not be able to put up with it for a little while. So what if I look like a diva badly in need of sleep. That's how the sultry look is done, I decide.

Looking at myself in the mirror, I realize I look more than half decent. At least nobody will mistake me for Farah's poor sidekick now.

'Ooh, someone's finally gotten out of her pyjamas,' Farah teases. 'I'd almost forgotten how hot you are.'

Her compliment makes me smile a little. We take a cab

to Blue Frog, one of my old-time favourite hangouts, and order our drinks.

We sit at the bar counter, waiting for the dance floor to warm up, and I notice a cute-ish guy eyeing Farah. She glances at him and smiles.

'Wanna talk to him?' I nudge.

'Not really. He's cute, but I'm done with men. I need a break,' she rolls her eyes. I smile knowingly.

I suddenly feel a knot build up inside my stomach, and my body breaks out in cold sweat. *Might be because I haven't drunk in a long time, and the air conditioner...* I think to myself.

'You don't look too good,' Farah says, looking at me.

What the hell is that supposed to mean. I spent an hour dressing up. One fuckin hour!

My intestines lurch and I can't hold it in any longer. I make a mad dash for the washroom, as a helpless and puzzled Farah looks on. The next few minutes feel like my innards will spill out into the toilet. *What on earth is happening?* I've barely had one drink! I stumble out of the washroom and make my way to the bar counter, my mind dazed and my vision totally blurred.

'Come on, quick,' Farah holds my arm and practically drags me out the door.

I am more than relieved to find a cab parked outside and before I can take a moment to appreciate Farah's presence of mind, she already tosses me in like a ragdoll. Coming out of a smoggy pub, the fresh air is some relief, but it does little to make the excruciating pain in my stomach go away. I begin to feel dizzy and the only thing I remember is Farah asking me to lie down on the back seat of the cab with my head in her lap.

My vision is still blurry when I open my eyes the next morning. I am in my bed, my hair neatly tied up and my party clothes changed into comfortable shorts and a tee. *How thoughtful of Farah...*

I try stumbling out of bed to make my way to the washroom, but my limbs feel weak and wobbly.

'Farah...' I squeak.

'I think she's up,' I hear Farah's voice from the living room outside. *Who is she talking to?*

'How are you feeling now?' she asks rushing into the room, looking concerned.

'Not too good. Wonder what's wrong...' I mumble.

'Let me check your blood pressure,' comes a deep voice and I look up to find Vivian standing in the room.

My mind spirals into a tizzy of thoughts and my heart... well...the lesser said of it, the better. A lot of it is déjà vu. Seeing his blurry face takes me back to that fateful day when I fell off a hotel balcony in Goa one crazy night and landed up in his hospital with a broken clavicle, which was how we met for the very first time. Oh God, he had looked so divine in that white coat. Well, he still looks divine, except that now he's the asshole who hanky-pankied with Aisha *and* then broke up with me.

A deluge of memories comes flooding back—that night of partying, me falling for him almost at first sight, and the many meetings between us that followed, which led us to a place where we were really looking forward to a future together. And he only had to do one thing to screw up all of it. *All of it!*

I can once again feel the anger bubbling within my depths, ready to explode.

'Of all the doctors in this big bad city, this is the only one you could find?!' I bellow at Farah, for lack of a better reaction.

'I'm sorry, Kay. But he was the only one I could think of at the moment. You were so sick and I panicked...'

I hrmph aloud and turn my head away towards the window, acutely aware of my childish behaviour. Farah had obviously meant well, but hell, this is awkward.

'Kay, can we talk about this later? You don't look too good,' Vivian says in a soft voice.

Of course I don't look too good. Do you expect me to look like a supermodel at eight in the morning!?

'He means you look ill, you idiot,' interrupts the Thought Bubble. *Of course I know that. I was just being sarcastic.*

I notice Vivian roll his eyes at me and that infuriates me even more. 'Why the hell are you here?' I bellow at him. 'I don't need you. I'll find another doctor. Farah, please ask him to leave. I just want to be left alone!'

'Yeah? How about I call that staircase kisser-boyfriend of yours? Maybe he'll be able to take better care of you,' Vivian shoots back.

It isn't like Vivian to be snarky and react like this. Or react at all. He is supposed to be the saintly one between the two of us.

'You are the one who goes about kissing idiots, not me,' I retort, instead of asking him what he means by that. My bitterness at him hooking up with Aisha overpowers every other feeling. And logic, in general.

And then it strikes me—Karan. Vivian was there when that total wet blanket of a kiss happened, if at all you could call it one.

'Karan is not my boyfriend!' I yell defiantly. How dare he accuse me of kissing people when he himself was an errant kisser?! 'In fact I *refused* the kiss. And it shouldn't even be any of your business because we had officially broken *off* and I was *single*, unlike *you*, when you kissed that…that *bitch*! And as a single *person*, I can kiss anyone *I like*!'

I realize that my intonation is all wonky, but what I don't realize is that yelling that loud is probably not such a great idea, because it makes the nerves in my head throb in a weird manner and before I know it, I can hear a faint siren wailing somewhere inside my head, and the world goes all blurry on me. Again.

A good few hours must have passed before I wake up, and who do I see sitting at my bedside? Jacinta! With Vivian standing right behind her. Nice touch, I think to myself. As if having him around wasn't bad enough, now there is a female version of him too.

'Do. Not. Say. A. Word. You have dengue and your BP. Is. Very. Low,' Jacinta says slowly but firmly, as if it is my IQ and not my BP she is talking about.

I wonder for a moment if dengue impacts intelligence in any way and whether I have indeed lost out on some grey cells. I know she doesn't think very highly of me, but she probably shouldn't be mean to me when I am sick in bed.

Still a bit dazed, I look around the room and spot Farah pottering about at the far end of the room, near the bookshelf, and Sherni comfortably perched on top of it.

'How come you're here?' I ask feebly, trying hard to sound polite and realizing that I don't have to make that effort, now that she isn't my sister-in-law-to-be anymore.

'Vivian called and said he needed me here,' she replies curtly.

I am not sure what she means, though. I look around for any signs of destruction, but everything is perfectly in place and the house is eerily silent. Ronan hasn't accompanied her this time, I infer.

It was probably the fight we had before I passed out that has led to this. Matters were clearly out of Vivian's control, and hence the big guns had to be pulled out. Jacinta had to be conjured.

This was probably his way of getting back at me, considering he knows how uncomfortable I am around his obnoxious sister. I feel extra bitter that he had to do this when I am half-dead from dengue.

'I thought you had surgeries lined up,' Jacinta shoots Vivian her classic look, a look that can turn water into icicles. He just nods sullenly and makes his way out of the room without uttering a word.

Oh God. Why did she have to send him away? What is she going to do to me now? I fumble around in the bed, attempting to sit up straight, when she places a hand on my leg.

No no no no no....

'So what's up with the two of you?' This woman is blunt as a butter knife, and obnoxiously demanding.

'We're not together anymore,' I reply curtly.

'You're going to make her very, very happy,' grins the Thought Bubble as I momentarily sulk at my own vulnerability. Jacinta does not like me one bit—she has made that pretty evident in the past.

I shoot Farah a look and she catches the cue and leaves immediately. Now that I am left alone with Jacinta in the room, my curiosity peaks further. *Why is she here?* It surely isn't out of love for me. I am not too sure how to broach the topic, though.

'Listen, you really need to give this some good hard thought. Vivian really loves you,' she says firmly, while I am still struggling internally with my thoughts and words.

'Wait...What?' I blurt out.

Jacinta has never been too hot on the idea of us. Then why is she trying to play Cupid and, must I admit, doing a spectacularly lame job of it?

Her eyes bore into mine as if she is privy to my thoughts. She clears her throat and readjusts herself into the chair.

'Look, Kay, I know I haven't exactly been...' she fumbles for words, her voice deliberately softened, but her ginormous ego showing in her stance.

'In favour of me and Vivian being together...' I butt in helpfully. The Thought Bubble groans haplessly in the background.

'It's not like that!' she protests weakly. She is so bad at faking emotions. Is there anything at all this woman can do well? 'Will you at least listen to me...'

Tired and weak from fever, I decide to sink back into the pillows and let her say whatever she has to.

'Vivian is my little brother, and I hate to admit, but the happiest I have seen him is whenever he is around you. And he may not show it, but he's been miserable since the two of you broke up. So if you still love him, please give it a thought. He really, really loves you.'

I feel something tug at the insides of my chest and rise up to sit in my throat. I wait for her to go on further, chiding her with my anticipation-filled eyes.

'That's all,' she says curtly.

Seriously? That's all? I am just beginning to get warmed up.

'I don't know what to say. He cheated on me. HE KISSED AISHA!' I yell, as if Aisha is the plague and kissing her is worst thing any living being can ever do. Which it so is.

Jacinta sits silent for a moment, presumably plotting a comeback.

'Deep in your heart you know that's not true,' she says matter-of-factly—such a loaded sentence, and yet completely devoid of drama.

'Hate her, but she's right,' whispers the Thought Bubble. I try to avert my gaze from her, but she holds it firm with her eyes, as if probing me for a response. For the umpteenth time, it dawns upon me that her eyes are the same shade of brown as Vivian's, and her nose has the same slant. Hell, it is like having a girl-version of Vivian sitting right before me.

'You have to mull this over, Kay. Don't ruin your life over a stupid mistake,' she concludes rather authoritatively and gets up to leave.

Her sense of entitlement over me never ceases to amaze me. I mean, her bossiness with Vivian is justified—she is his big sister. But what have I done to deserve her weight being thrown upon me?

My heartbeats slowly pace down to normal after she leaves, and my mind feels strangely calmer. This isn't the typical effect Jacinta has on me—that friggin' nerve cyclone. But this time—as much as I hate to admit, and despite our mutual dislike for each other—I know she is right, and that she means well. It must've taken her a big heart, and probably some hallucinogens, to actually come all the way to Mumbai and play the unwilling peacenik, when she could've easily caused more damage.

I have to see Vivian. Now.

'But you can barely walk!' Farah protests when I inform her that I'll have to leave for the hospital.

'I think I'm fine,' I retort bravely as I gulp down a glass of Glucose mix to rev up my engine. I can easily last a couple of hours on this, I tell myself.

Have you ever been fascinated by how time and speed are such relative entities? The cab can't move any slower.

'Have you thought over what you'll say to him?' asks the Thought Bubble innocuously. I gulp a little. Of course I haven't. I've just hauled myself out of bed, pulled on a pair of jeans and a clean tee and plonked myself into a cab. I really haven't thought this through. What will I say to him? How will he respond? After all that has happened between the two of us, will he even want to talk to me? Anxiety grips my heart as I get off the cab and make my way to his cabin on the first floor of the hospital.

'Ma'am, Dr Vivian just stepped out for a while,' the pudgy receptionist informs me with a weird look about her face as I proceed to turn the doorknob. The staff here knows me well, for I used to drop in often in happier times and circumstances. She is probably stumped to see me walk in so abruptly, because I haven't visited in months.

I must admit, I am partially relieved to hear that he isn't in—mostly because I am not mentally prepared for the confrontation that is to ensue. Maybe it is all for the best. This is not the time for it. Questions will fly, arguments will follow, mistakes will be dug out from their graves and there will be a whole lot of emotional drama that I'd perhaps be better-equipped to deal with without the dengue weighing me down.

At the same time, I can feel impatience pulsating through

my veins. However dreadful it is going to be, and despite the uncertainty of it all, I really want to have that talk with Vivian. I want to understand what he wants. I want to know if his feelings for me have changed in the past few months. I want to know if we still stand a chance. 'We'. I haven't thought of us as a 'we' in quite a while now. Or maybe I have—fleetingly. Every time I found thoughts of us being together creep into my mind, in memories or in dreams, I would push them out with all my might. I just wasn't ready to let Vivian in. But in this moment, something has changed. I'm not sure whether it is Jacinta's rather-curt advice or the healing that comes with time—when you are no longer in the eye of the storm, but have walked far enough to be able to look at the storm more objectively and dispassionately. Or maybe it is the fever messing with my brain functions. Whatever it is, I know I want to be with Vivian, and after the longest time, I have no qualms in admitting that I hope he wants to be with me too.

'Madam, do you want to go somewhere?' the cabbie interrupts my fast-spiralling-out-of-control confusion. Lost in thoughts, I didn't realize that I have walked out of the hospital and onto the road. And I begin feeling light-headed too.

'Get home right away and mull it over in bed,' quips the Thought Bubble, and for once I am all too eager to take its advice. The sweltering Mumbai heat is certainly not helping my cause and all the noise from the traffic and the people walking by is only adding to my disorientation. Also, my heart isn't about to listen to my mind. I turn back and begin walking back towards the hospital.

His evening shift is a couple of hours away, and this is the best place to catch hold of him.

'Oh, you're back, madam?' quips Rita, his secretary, as I saunter back into the reception area. I nod briefly and plonk myself into one of the sofas there, almost tempted to put my feet up and lie down.

'Can I get you something?' she asks again.

'A blanket please, if you can,' I reply meekly.

A part of me wants to go home and hibernate, but that part of me is much weaker than the part of me that wants to sort things out with Vivian. Now. Rita obliges and fetches a blanket from the storage cabinet. Once I ease into its warmth, it doesn't take me long to drift into sleep.

It is six in the evening when I wake up, and there is still no sign of Vivian. 'Is he not going to come in today?' I ask Rita, trying to sound nonchalant even though my innards are fluttering in anxiety. It has been five freakin' hours and my body is begging for mercy...and a proper bed.

'I don't know. I've been trying to call him, but his phone is switched off,' Rita shrugs.

It isn't like him at all to switch off his phone. He has patients calling him at odd hours of the day, and often at night too; he always makes sure he is available for them.

And then he saunters in. His hair dishevelled, his eyelids droopy and his white shirt sloppily hanging out over the belt of his trousers. Just to put this in context—Vivian never ever lets his shirt hang out like that. Ever. In fact, I remember having arguments with him over this, because he would even tuck in his T-shirts into his bermudas and clamp it over with a leather belt—even when we were out on a walk or lounging by the beach. I mean, who dresses so tight and proper all the time?

'He looks like he's just walked out of a cyclone,' remarks the Thought Bubble. I saw him just that morning, and he looked perfectly fine. What on earth could have hit him? Wait a minute—has he caught the dengue bug too?

'Vivian, what the...?' I start off, completely forgetting my script. I have thought of so many things I want to say to him, but looking at his beaten-down and weary face, I lose track of them.

Rita and the other hospital staff are now throwing carefully confused, yet quite obviously bemused looks our way. But Vivian doesn't seem one bit fazed. He has an IDGAF look on his face—one that I have never seen him wearing before. He always gives a fuck. About everything.

'Wait a minute. Are you drunk!?' I exclaim as he stumbles closer.

His pupils are fixed wide and his eyes look glazed over.

'Yeah, I am. So?' he replies defiantly. 'And what are you doing here?'

Something about his tone tells me that this isn't going to be pleasant.

'Want to step into your cabin?' I gesture at him with a raised eyebrow, but in his inebriated state, I doubt he'll even catch my not-so-subtle hint.

Vivian. The always-so-prim-and-propah, having-his-shit-together Vivian. I just can't wrap my head around the fact that he just walked into the hospital looking like that.

'You...you ruined everything!' His speech is slurred and I know that if he speaks for a second longer, he won't be able to step into this hospital ever again with his head held high.

Despite my aching muscles, I grab him by the torso and drag him into his cabin. He can unleash whatever drama he wants to in here, without the baggage of future embarrassment.

'What is wrong with you, Vivian!?' I ask him sternly. 'This is so not you!'

'Oh yeah? And what you did was supposed to be you? Mistrusting me and then moving on to another guy even before I had a chance to clear things up. Is that what we were about, Kay?' His voice is low and shaky and just plain weird.

Anything I say right now will hit the wall, because clearly, he isn't thinking straight. Moreover, I don't really know what to say. I have made a mistake. He has made a mistake. Now, it is up to both of us to walk that distance and meet midway.

'Vivian... I...' I begin, not sure where I am going to take this conversation. There is so much to be said, but I struggle to put it into words. But much to my surprise, he makes it easier for me—he passes out on his couch.

Back home, the room looks messier than what it was when I'd walked out, but I am left with no energy to clean it up. The fatigue is more mental than physical. I can't wait for the day to end so I can go right up to Vivian's house and shoot away all the questions that are bubbling inside me. I just hope that he is back to his senses by then and not too hungover to have a conversation.

'Oh, you are back home already?' Farah chirps as she walks past my room. She is chirpy and glowing, quite unlike my sallow face with fever-matted hair. Looking at her freshly showered self almost motivates me to take one myself. Almost. I groan and throw myself back on the heap of pillows at the far end of the bed.

'Take a shower, maybe? It might make you feel better?' she says casually, as if reading my thoughts.

Do I really look that shabby? I look at myself in the mirror at the far end of the room and infer that I kinda do. And to think that I went all the way to meet Vivian at the hospital looking like this. I am probably all smelly like a wet dog, and that's probably why my bedsheet smells funky too.

Farah's disapproving look gives me the courage to once again haul my weight out of the comfort of my bed and make my way to the washroom. And truth be told, the warm water is quite an antidote for my frayed nerves and overanxious mind. I stay under the shower for a long-ish while, gathering my thoughts and feeling more ready to take on the BIG TALK I am going to have with Vivian. I play multiple scenarios in my head and have them all covered with appropriate comebacks.

I feel a tinge of hesitation as I make my way to Vivian's apartment in the evening. I haven't told him that I will come, and I just hope he is home and willing to talk things out like a sane person. It seems like a long time since I last walked out of his house, and yet, it feels like it was just yesterday. We hadn't spent too much time under the same roof, but it had begun to feel like home. It just didn't feel the same after I came back to my turf—even though I have spent several years living here. It dawns on me that home is not a place, it is a person. And for me, Vivian is home.

I make my way up the elevator to his apartment, and hanging on the door is a sign that says, in big bold letters—'WELCOME HOME, KAY'.

My eyes tear up. The varnish fumes from the woodwork going on in the neighbour's house might have something to do with it too, but hey. Even before I can press the bell, the door swings open, and Vivian stands there, in his familiar night tee and sweatpants. Just like me, he looks freshly showered. 'I knew you would come,' he says with a smile.

I am almost at a loss for words, but I have to say all those things I have been rehearsing in my head for so long. 'Let's talk?' I say in a broken voice.

'I have a better idea,' he says and pulls me close to him, looking straight into my eyes.

Without a second thought, our lips find each other and what follows is perhaps the longest, most intense and tear-laden kiss in the history of our relationship. The varnish fumes are partly to blame, but truth be told, I haven't felt this alive and relieved in the longest time.

Epilogue

*B*efore there is scope for anything else to go wrong, Vivian and I finalize a wedding date—nothing fancy, just a court do and a cosy brunch with family and close friends over the weekend. I wear a gorgeous white-and-gold saree that my mom picked out for me, and Vivian wears a white silk kurta in which he looks dapper—as ever. We stand there before the registrar with wide grins plastered across our faces. *We have made it and nothing can go wrong now.*

Just then my phone rings. 'Baani's water broke this morning. We won't be able to come,' Kapil yells from the other end.

'OMG, Kapil! This is the best wedding gift you guys could have ever given me!' I beam. Just the thought of becoming an aunty doubles my happiness.

'Kay! What's wrong with you! I am losing my shit here!' Kapil yells. His voice is panicky and he is huffing and puffing, as if he himself has gone into labour. Trust Kapil to go all dramatic at the wrong times.

'Where is Baani?' I ask coolly.

'She's in the labour room!' he shrieks.

'It's the labour room, Kapil. Not the ER. CALM THE FUCK DOWN,' I shriek back.

And that's how our wedding goes. We quickly sign on the papers, exchange a quick hug and a kiss and hop into our car to drive straight to Goa! Luckily, we had packed in a few clothes because we had planned to spend our wedding night in a hotel.

Being married to Vivian makes me happy, but what makes me infinitely happier is seeing my Baani with her beautiful baby girl. She looks like the most precious thing on the planet and I am so relieved that her face has taken after Baani and not Kapil. I mean Kapil is not ugly or anything, just that...well...

We quickly adapt our honeymoon plans to the situation and decide to stay on in Goa for a few more days. I could have never imagined how nostalgic it would feel to revisit all those places where our love had blossomed, starting from that hospital in Calangute.

Meanwhile in Mumbai, Ravi and Farah develop some kind of a weird chemistry that seems like more than a casual hookup. They have been hanging out an awful lot and I am getting to see a side of Ravi that I have never seen before—the gentlemanly side. I guess that's what love does to you—it makes you a better person.

And as for Aisha, she is still around, and will probably always be, but I promised myself to never ever let myself fall for her evil antics again. If there is anything that I have learnt over the past few months, it is that in tough times, it's not love and romance that see you through—it is the trust you have in each other.

But am I done with love? Not yet, I guess!

Acknowledgements

Let me begin with where it all started: Ayzel, my daughter, after who Kairavi is named—both the names mean 'moonlight'. She is the one who fills up my life with love and inspiration.

My family, who has stood firm like a rock beside me, at every single turn.

Amit, my friend, mentor and guide. And my go-to person for everything.

Suhail Mathur, my agent, who showed faith in this book when nobody else did.

My team at work, for being so sweet and supportive in every possible way.

The wonderful folks at Rupa, who worked so hard to give this book its shape and form.

My friends, who are also my biggest cheerleaders—you know who you are.